# BILL, THE GALACTIC HERO

## THE FINAL INCOHERENT ADVENTURE!

# BILL, THE GALACTIC HERO

## THE FINAL INCOHERENT ADVENTURE!

# HARRY HARRISON
## AND DAVID M. HARRIS

Artwork by Mark Pacella

A Byron Preiss Book

AVON BOOKS • NEW YORK

BILL, THE GALACTIC HERO: THE FINAL INCOHERENT ADVENTURE! is an original publication of Avon Books. This work has never before appeared in book form. This work is a novel. Any similarity to actual persons or events is purely coincidental.

Special thanks to Nat Sobel, Henry Morrison, Dainis Bisenieks, and Chris Miller.

For Jenny Mershon, Bettina Harris, and Shelley Rochester.
Better late than never.
Special thanks to Kate Myslinski.

AVON BOOKS
A division of
The Hearst Corporation
1350 Avenue of the Americas
New York, New York 10019

BILL, THE GALACTIC HERO: THE FINAL INCOHERENT ADVENTURE! copyright © 1992 by Byron Preiss Visual Publications, Inc.
Illustrations copyright © 1992 by Byron Preiss Visual Publications, Inc.
Published by arrangement with Byron Preiss Visual Publications, Inc.
Cover and book design by Alex Jay/Studio J
Edited by John Betancourt
Front cover painting by Mark Pacella and Steve Fastner
Library of Congress Catalog Card Number: 91-92412
ISBN: 0-380-75667-6

First AvoNova Printing: September 1992

AVONOVA TRADEMARK REG. U.S. PAT. OFF. AND IN OTHER COUNTRIES, MARCA REGISTRADA, HECHO EN U.S.A.

Printed in the U.S.A.

RA   10   9   8   7   6   5   4   3   2   1

# BILL, THE GALACTIC HERO

## THE FINAL INCOHERENT ADVENTURE!

# CHAPTER 1

FEET. FEET OF ALL SORTS AND SHAPES AND sizes. A whole foot locker full of feet. There were feet that looked like standard issue Trooper's boots and there were feet that looked like running shoes and there were feet that looked like stainless steel wing-tips. There were even feet that looked like they came from all sorts of repulsive animals, like bowb-beavers and regurgibirds. There was even one that looked like that of a rusty robo-mule, just for sentiment's sake. Why there were even feet that looked like sports cars, and space ships, and the feet of some of Bill's favorite holo-cartoon characters. The foot locker was really a feetlocker, for it held every kind of foot you could think of, and some you couldn't, everything but real feet. They were all artificial feet. Bill's feet.

Feet had been a problem for a long time for Bill—ever since he'd been stuck on Veneria, the death planet, and had to shoot off his foot to get off that planet. In this man's war there was always a shortage of replacement feet. In the fullness of time he'd wound up with an elephant foot, a satyr foot, a mood foot—more feet than he could remember. Now he had even more feet than that, and all at once. He had finally given up even trying to get a real human foot for a replacement: a shiny socket now sprang from his truncated ankle.

*Snap.* He glared at the black lacquered one with the red and gold pagoda? No, not for tonight. He needed something a lot snazzier if he was going to get anywhere near a woman on this pass. *Snap.* Bill rummaged through the trunk for a foot with more sex appeal. Maybe the pink plush number with the bright red curly plastic toenails? *Snap.* No. Not macho enough. *Snap.* Yes, here's the one! *Snap.* Bill stepped back to admire his choice in the small mirror at the foot of his bunk.

This was a foot to reckon with, a foot that said "here strides a man of parts," even if he hadn't been born with all the same parts he had now. It was big and hairy and wild, just like Bill imagined he was, and very ape-like—really like Bill. This was the mother, if not the father, of all feet.

It was early evening at Camp Buboe, and Bill had, through a delicate combination of bribery, extortion, and shaking the company clerk by the throat, acquired a pass from this same clerk. Considering that the town outside the base to which this pass entitled him to go was distinguishable from the base principally because it was on the other side of a fence, this might not be such a big deal. But there were rumored to be women there, women who did not wear the olive drab of the Imperial Troopers, women who sat in bars where alcoholic beverages were served in quantities, women who might be spoken to and touched and—Bill began panting and had to restrain his fevered imagination.

Off in the distance, a commotion was stirring. Bill turned his combat-trained senses to the front of the barracks, and heard the cry, "Officer coming!" His combat-honed reflexes had him instantly heading for the back door and safety.

Too late. He stormed out the back door into a brick wall.

No, not exactly a brick wall. He was sure he would have remembered a wall just outside the door, and even at Camp Buboe the walls didn't wear uniforms. But Sergeant Brickwall was even bigger than Bill, and he knew a fleeing Trooper when he saw one.

Bill stopped cold, then bared his treasured fangs at the sergeant and growled deep in his throat.

Brickwall bared his own implanted, sharpened incisors and growled back, like a murderous vampire bunny.

Bill roared, and shook drool from his fangs into the sergeant's face.

Brickwall roared back, and shook Bill's own drool back at him, with some of his own for interest.

Bill roared again, and pounded his chest.

Brickwall did the same, and flashed his fangs again.

Clearly, subtlety was getting Bill nowhere.

"Move your fat bowby body," he bellowed.

Brickwall laughed in a most insulting manner.

"Your mother wears combat boots!" Bill sneered sneeringly.

Brickwall blinked. "Of course!" he foamed indignantly. "She's a Trooper. What else should she wear?"

"Your teeth look stupid!" Bill screamed in desperation. "Rabbits are full of bowb—and who's afraid of rodent vegetarians?"

Brickwall gnashed the offenders at Bill.

Diplomacy wasn't working either.

"Ehhhh, what's up, Bill?"

"Be a buddy, Buddy," Bill burbled. In a sudden spasm of desperation he flung himself to the ground and grappled his arms around the sergeant's knees. "Please don't make me go back in there. There's an *officer* in the barracks. Something awful is sure to happen." But even this pathetic appeal didn't help.

"Sorry, Bill, but you know the rules: cover your ass.

If I let anyone out I have to go in myself. You can't forget the Trooper's code."

Indeed Bill could not. It was ingrained in them all, from the rawest recruit to the most senior non-com: hypnotically drilled into their brains.

*Every week is bowb-your-buddy week.*

"It's been nice knowing you, Bill. Can I have your fangs when you get killed?"

Bill was too depressed even to answer this routine request. He hauled himself to his feet, made a quick feint to see if he could get past the sergeant, bounced back well crunched, then plodded gloomily back into the barracks. This was a depressing place at the best of times, carefully designed by the emperor's sister-in-law in colors guaranteed to keep morale at a steady low level and the stomach at the point of regurgitation. Now not even Bill's collection of feet could cheer him up.

And it only got worse. The officer who had come in was a short, scrawny man, flanked by six tall, extraordinary-proportioned female bodyguards. This could be none other than Captain Kadaffi, hero of the Emperor's Own Household Commandos. He had survived dozens of battles, scores of raids behind enemy lines, and countless assassination attempts by his own Troopers. He was known and admired, only by other officers of course, for his willingness to stay in a battle to the very end, until the last enlisted men had been killed.

The enlisted men didn't admire that part so much, but their opinions didn't count. They were the ones who had tried to assassinate him, after all. They even tried to take him out when he was lecturing them, the motto being "a frag in class may save your ass."

The bodyguards formed up in a semicircle around Kadaffi, flaunting guns and blasters at the ready. The captain struck a pose that was only slightly less macho than that of the women. "I need volunteers!" he squeaked with officerial authority.

Bill and the other Troopers shuffled their feet and tried

to back away. The bodyguards' blasters twitched and there were a few warning shots fired into the barracks ceiling.

"I need twenty red-blooded heroes! Now is there anyone here who doesn't have red blood?" The Troopers tried to come up with a good answer to that one, but Kadaffi didn't give them time. "Right—you all volunteer."

The officer wheeled and disappeared behind the bodyguards. The biggest of them, a redhead of terrifying voluptuousness, stepped forward and covered the men. "Grab your gear and fall in. Now!" She punctuated the order by flirtatiously firing a few rounds into the floor at Bill's feet.

"Hey," he protested, "that's one of my best feet!"

"You won't need it where you're going. You won't need it at all after tonight. Too bad, too. That's a kinda' sexy foot, buster."

"Not Buster, Bill. With two l's, just like an officer." But the redhead had already lost interest.

The feet locker lay open like a treasure chest, but its temptations meant nothing to Bill now. He reached down to the bottom and pulled out the foot he hated, the one he never wanted to wear—the Swiss Army Foot.

This was a masterpiece of the foot-designer's art. It was the top of the line in high-tech feet, with special attachments and hidden weapons and secret compartments. There was a poisoned knife that shot out of the toe, a mini-laser that could be used for welding or for shooting people, a dart gun, an ammunition box, a toolkit, a condom dispenser, a small bottle of hot sauce, a length of super-strong monofilament line, a compass, a flare gun, a collapsible mess kit, a saw, a corkscrew, a magnifying glass, and a bunch of other things, some of which he had to read the manual to find out about because he had forgotten. The manual had more words than pictures, and was about the same size as the foot as well, so Bill had never read it very much. It didn't much matter, since the only one of all those tools and attachments Bill had used so far was the bottle of hot sauce. Though unhappily the hot sauce had eaten a large hole through the instant imitation field-combat food-type product, improving it immensely. The packaging, that is. The food was still inedible.

The combat foot was also very large. It was a good thing it was lightened by all the compartments, or it would have been too heavy to walk with.

With the combat foot snapped securely onto his ankle socket, Bill looked around desperately for something else to take with him into combat, and maybe, of course, into the Great Beyond. It was taken for granted that everything he had ever owned that was of sentimental value, every reminder of his home on Phigerinadon IV, had long ago been lost. Even the holo-snapshot of his robomule was gone. Wiping away a small tear with his left-right hand—that was his only memento of his old shipmate the Voodoo minister and Fusetender Sixth Class Reverend Tembo (as opposed to his other right hand, which was original equipment)—Bill jammed his Imperial-issue hat on top of his Imperial-issue head and prepared to meet his Imperial-issue doom.

As they exited, a squad of heavily armed Troopers fell in around the volunteers to make absolutely sure none of them escaped, then escorted them to the armory. Armored combat jump suits awaited them; they had no choice but to climb in.

Actually, these suits had a lot in common with Bill's foot. They were made by the same company (The Emperor's Second Cousin's Own Defense Company, Inc.) with the same care and attention to detail. They both had lots of fancy features and attachments that worked really well sometimes, and hardly at all most of the time. They had the same scuffed, chipped, imitation pseudo-chrome finish. .

And they were all about the same size.

Bill realized pretty quickly that the foot wasn't going to go inside the suit. He made a big show of trying to get it in, making sure that Captain Kadaffi and his bodyguards saw him.

He pushed and twisted and made funny noises.

"Unk!" he unked.

"Krskq!" he krskqed.

It was an elaborate and impressive performance. He jumped and spun and pirouetted and did a credible imitation of a man diving off a tower into a fish tank. Throwing out the top and bottom scores, the other volunteers gave him a 9 out of 15. Captain Kadaffi was not impressed. He ordered the big redhead over to see what was going on.

"What games you playing at, bowbhead?" she sighed.

"My foot won't go into the suit." She bent down to look at the problem, and Bill caught an intoxicating whiff of something—gun oil? His pulse raced and his loins throbbed. "I guess I can't go with you after all. Not if I can't get into the suit, right?"

"Wrong. I'm going to shoot that foot off."

"You can't! This is my combat foot," Bill shouted in panic. "Top of the line." He thought about it for a second. "On the other hand," he said smarmily, "if you'd like to let me go back to my bunk, I might be able to pick out a replacement in just a few hours." He inhaled her scent again. "Maybe afterwards we could go someplace private and get familiar with each other's feet."

"No way, big boy." She shook her head. "Not that it isn't tempting, but you're a commando now. You know the slogan—The Few, The Proud, The Dead. Doesn't pay for me to get involved with commandos."

The redhead bent over the suit again. "Here's the problem." She pulled out a laser cutter and sliced off the suit boot. "That ought to do it. Your foot's not too bad a match, and now you can use it in combat, and, what the hell, you will be dead soon anyway. Everyone's happy, right?"

Bill clicked his foot off, jammed his leg down into the suit, then clamped his combat foot back on. The bodyguard taped the suit leg to the foot with some duct tape and slapped him on the back. "Congratulations, old buddy, you're going to die a glorious death in the service of the Emperor. I'd like to be with you, but I have to stay with Captain Kadaffi in the rear. Better well fed than long dead."

Bill shrugged his understanding and started checking out his weapons. Laser cannon, fully charged. Grenade rack and launcher, loaded and ready. Armor, chipped and pitted, but not too leaky. Machine pistols, loaded. He swung up one of the guns to fire off a couple of test rounds in the general direction of Kadaffi's left ventricle.

*Click. Click.* Nothing happened.

Except the captain squealed with delight. "Excellent!"

He swaggered over to Bill, who was now surrounded by lethal feminine pulchritude and quivering in antici-pation of an extremely messy and sudden demise.

"What happened?" Bill asked.

"*This* happened," Kadaffi said with a flourish, pulling out a small device that looked like a holovision remote control. "My remote control, that's what. You don't think I'd be crazy enough to stay in a room full of armed Troopers, do you? None of your weapons will work until *I* say so.

"But you, my boy," he said, grinning obnoxiously up at Bill, "you have showed initiative.

"You shall have the honor of leading the attack."

Bill contemplated his new honor with growing horror.

"Oh, bowb," he muttered, still clicking the unfunctioning trigger.

# CHAPTER 2

IT WAS DARK INSIDE THE BELLY OF THE AT-tack transport. The constant vibration of the engines kept the troopers' stomachs churning noisily at a level just above full heartburn and a little below outright up-chucking. Which at least distracted them from the deadly attack to come. A low moaning came from the rear.

Bill was sitting up front, in the no-moaning section. The door to the first class cabin had been open a teensy crack when they came aboard, though it had very quickly been slammed shut. He was still hoping vainly for a second glimpse at this military paradise. The first had been tantalizing, a hint of all the heady pleasures reserved for officers: the magenta and puce velvet-upholstered couches, the strains of classical jew's-harp music, the elegant original black-velvet artwork, the clink and gurgling of something undoubtedly alcoholic being poured over ice, the bodyguards dropping their weapons and starting to unbutton . . . and then the door had been kicked shut. Bill didn't care for ice—it diluted the booze when it melted—but all the rest was akin to

9

heaven. Since he might very well be going to that Trooper's valhalla in a little while, it seemed only fair that he should have a taste now.

With a burst of light and ear-hurting static the front wall of the transport hold sprang to life in glorious black-and-white. A scattered image of Captain Kadaffi slowly gathered itself together. He was reading myopically from a piece of paper.

"As we head together into glorious battle in the Emperor's name I want you all to know that the hearts of free humans everywhere are here with you at this stupendous moment," he read in an obnoxious nasal whine. "We are engaged in a terrible battle against the godless"—and here the image paused while another voice filled in, 'Chingers'—"in which the future of civilization itself is at stake. The Emperor himself wants you to know that your sacrifice will not be in vain. Your names will be recorded in the Emperor's Own Big Book of the Glorious Dead. If, by any mistake, any of you happens to survive, he will be given a medal and a twelve-hour pass."

The captain looked at the paper with disgust, then hurled it aside. "Yeah, yeah. There's a lot more bowb about glory and patriotism and so on. Blah, blah, blah. Now here's your mission."

The recorded image wavered and was replaced by a new one, in color. Some of the troopers actually looked up at it and almost started paying some attention. Only because one of the bodyguards, a blonde with long, flowing hair, and an open blouse, leaned over Kadaffi's shoulders and blew kisses at the troopers along with revealing a fine display of her cleavage. His eyes crossed as he tried to see the view—then he snapped back to attention.

"We, and of course I mean *you*, should be reaching the drop zone in a few minutes. There's a big battle down there. You don't need to know where it is or what it's about. Other than that we're coming in behind the

Chinger lines in a sneak suicide attack. You're a diversion from the main attack. All you have to do is get on the ground and shoot everything that moves. Try not to kill each other, although it won't matter much.

"You there, Trooper Bill—you're the point man. You other guys will follow Bill forward into glorious combat. Introduce yourself, Bill."

Bill raised a reluctant hand; no one bothered to look.

"Thanks, Bill. I want you all to know that I'll be behind you all the way. Far behind. Of course, I'll do it all by remote control from right here, but someone has to get back to tell the story of your courage, right? Right." The blonde ran her hand through Kadaffi's hair. "So long, loyal Troopers." He yawned and turned away, already forgetting them.

The picture blinked out, then blinked back on. It was almost the same, except the blonde had two more buttons undone. Kadaffi scratched his head and tried to take his eyes off the view. "I forgot to tell you that you better get ready to jump. You might not get much warning." The wall faded back to its own airsick yellow.

All around Bill, troopers were fastening their helmets and gloves, sealing their face plates, rechecking their ammo, writing their wills, emptying their stomachs.

They were in some planet's atmosphere now because they could hear the sounds of combat outside the transport. Judging by the explosions, lots of very unfortunate things were happening not very far away. Some of the blasts were very large. Some things were blowing up. In fact, *lots* of things were blowing up, some of them pretty close.

The transport started swerving and swaying and twisting and banking to stay away from the anti-aircraft fire. Which was a good idea, only it did not work very well. For suddenly there was no floor any more.

In that first instant Bill hoped that the floor had been shot away, not retracted. Because that might mean that

Captain Kadaffi was not safe and might be wasted along with the rest of them.

Then Bill was plummeting through space.

He screamed for a while, but it didn't seem to help. He kept on plummeting. He went through "Oh bowb, oh bowb!" and "I don't wanna die!" and "Heeeeelp!" and even "Mommy!", but he just kept falling. He tried activating the antigravity unit in his suit, but that was linked to the same remote control as the weapons, back up in Captain Kadaffi's hot little hand. Or cold little hand since he might be dead and that would be the end of that.

At last Bill tried looking down.

Well, it wasn't as bad an idea as he'd thought it might be. He was still plummeting, but he couldn't see the ground, only clouds. It didn't really feel like falling, except for the wind, and he could hear that, but not feel it. Sealed in the suit he couldn't feel much of anything. He could see out the face plate, and he could smell the sweat—and was that blood?—of the last guy who'd worn it, but he couldn't feel anything.

He looked around and saw the rest of the volunteers. Their radios were remotely controlled as well, so all they could do was wave to each other and plummet, which they did for quite a while.

Then they broke through the clouds.

They were seen at once and the firing started. Bullets and shells and laser blasts whizzed around them—but the entire squad was falling so fast by this time that no one could draw a bead on them.

But the squad could see just fine. And what they could see was lots and lots of tiny little figures that were getting larger very fast. The little figures were pointing up at the plummeting troopers and shooting at them. But the good Captain Kadaffi had other things to think about and hadn't pushed the button on his remote control yet. They couldn't shoot back. All they could do, really, was fall, and they were getting very good at that.

Bill didn't think they needed any more practice at falling. Even he, dense as he was from time to time, had mastered the falling technique in the first few seconds. Of course, there was always the possibility that this was their entire mission. A trooper in an armored combat suit weighed quite a lot, and could probably destroy a small building if he scored a direct hit on it. But that would probably destroy the suit, and suits were expensive—much more so than Troopers. So the captain had probably just forgotten to turn on the antigrav units. That was reassuring. Some.

Bill tried to relax and enjoy the descent and be ready for whatever happened next. Much to his surprise, that turned out to be an abrupt yank upwards, driving all of the lower part of the suit into his crotch.

When he regained consciousness, he was wafting gently downward toward the waiting arms of the enemy. They weren't waiting very patiently. They were sending up a lot of stuff to welcome him, and judging by how it exploded, it wasn't an entirely friendly welcome. And they were getting the range.

Bill looked down at a whole army trying to kill him. He looked up toward the transport, where only one man was trying to kill him.

He figured his odds and made his decision. Kadaffi was more of a threat.

He reached up and felt the helmet. The big antenna would be for the remote control. The middle-sized one would be for the radio to the other troopers, if that ever worked. The little one—here it was!—would be the locater beacon. He got a good grip on it and yanked, but the designers had planned for that, and it did not budge. Even with both hands, he couldn't break it off. He could blast it with his gun, but he didn't want to risk destroying the antigrav unit, or, for that matter, his head.

If only he could get to his Swiss Army Foot! He twisted around until he could reach his foot, tore off the duct tape, and pressed the button that released the tool kit. It was a little gizmo, small enough to fit in his hand, with various tools that folded out of the sides. Small knife, nail file, large knife, scissors, awl, flat-head screwdriver, Phillips-head screwdriver, bottle opener, can opener—where the bowb was it? At last he found what he was looking for—the portable foldout bolt cutter. In an instant he had the antenna sliced off and discarded.

Now that bowbhead Captain Kadaffi couldn't tell where Bill was.

Bill started firing his machine guns at the enemy. He didn't care if he hit anything, but the recoil would push him in the other direction. He started drifting away from the action, but the wind was against him, and he was still going down. By now he was wreathed in smoke and completely alone. Pretty soon now he'd be locked in combat, with the enemy really aiming at him, instead of just shooting blindly. Not at all what he had in mind.

First he used up the rest of his machine-gun ammo. That reduced his weight some, enough to slow down his descent, but not enough to stop it entirely. Then he dropped all his grenades, hoping that there was no one below who would be hit by one. He didn't want to get anyone irritated, especially anyone with a blaster. Still not enough weight, though.

The gloves with the built-in blasters were next. Then the backpack with the dehydrated water pills, fresh disposable underwear made of recycled toilet paper that could also be used as toilet paper, pseudo-meal pills, and Imperial issue last effects. He was still falling slowly.

The armored combat boot may have injured someone when it dropped, and his armored trousers left a small crater. Now Bill was low enough to see the ground— and the gunners on the ground could see him.

But by now he was only drifting slowly towards the ground. He loosened his belt and let fly. His armored pants dropped and thudded to the ground and Bill was flying steady.

Except that the wind was still pushing him over the enemy lines but, with his underwear fluttering proudly in the breeze and his arms held resolutely over his head, Bill hoped that he might be pretty safe. And he seemed to be right. No one was shooting at him, not even the other troopers.

He could see them now, floating below him and well ahead, slipping into a formation for attack. As long as he wasn't involved it looked kind of interesting. They formed into a wedge—with an empty spot at the front where he was supposed to be—and charged into the enemy lines.

Of course, they were charging *down*, too, and Bill was going down with them. Captain Kadaffi might not have known where Bill was, but he was sure trying to get him killed anyway.

What else could he drop to lighten his weight? His boot was already gone along with his pants. Bill really hoped he wouldn't have to drop his combat foot; he had no idea when he might be able to find a replacement, and he'd spent altogether too much time without a foot on that leg in the last few years.

He did take the foot off, though. The small combat laser built into the Swiss Army Foot was powerful enough to cut away pieces of the remaining armor. Bit by bit, he carved away the entire upper half of the combat suit, sparing only the helmet and the antigrav unit. Taking the straps from the back-mounted antigrav pack in his teeth, he shrugged out of the rest of the outfit.

Ah, stable flight again. Looping the straps through his shorts, he relaxed and watched what he could see of the action below. Which wasn't much, although it looked like the suicide mission was working out as planned. Suicidal. The Imperial Troopers were getting but creamed. For a fleeting instant Bill felt sorry for his former comrades. But the sensation faded quickly and he wished he had some of those dehydrated beer pills.

Bill had been in more than his share of battles, but

he'd never had a chance to pay much attention to one before. When you're in the middle of the action, it makes even less sense than it does from the generals' point of view, which was pretty dim at best. There was always a lot of noise and confusion and, of course, people shooting at you. This means you keep your head down and don't see very much. In fact, the less you see, generally speaking, the better. If you can see the enemy, they can see you. For that matter, it's a good idea to stay out of sight of your own side when the bulk of a Trooper's training was how to obey orders and clean latrines. How to aim and shoot various weapons was just an afterthought. Bill had learned how to use a blaster long ago, but he'd done it by reading the Official Imperial Trooper Comix version of the manual. Then he got a lot of practice on Veneria and various other challenging and deadly planets.

But no matter how good he got at gunning down officers and other enemies, he never got the full satisfaction of warfare, of knowing that his work was worthwhile and appreciated, that it was part of some larger effort. Sure, the news comix told all about how the Troopers were sweeping the Chingers from all the planets of the galaxy, but they seemed to keep sweeping them from the same planets all the time. From the ground, which Bill spent a lot of time staying very close to in combat, there didn't appear to be any pattern to it at all.

From here, though, it was all different. Up here in the air with his shorts flapping jauntily in the breeze, waving gaily to the troops on both sides below and wondering where the closest bar might be, Bill could see the whole battle spread out like a map. The Chinger forces were arranged in a long, thin, green rectangle, just like in the news comix, and the Imperial troops were coming at them in the shapes of big, curved red arrows. It wasn't the best way to win a battle, but it did look good on the air reconnaissance photos that the general staff had to send to the Emperor.

The two big arrows moved forward and back, forward and back again, not making much progress toward anything, but getting a little bit smaller each time as the points were blasted away.

A small white arrow was poking ineffectually at the other side of the green rectangle, getting a lot of attention from the green gunners. Bill couldn't tell if any of the volunteers were still alive, because Captain Kadaffi's remote control wasn't concerned with that. The little box just kept the suits in formation so they could be blasted more easily. The captain might not even have been paying attention, as long as that arrow stayed neat and pointed in the right direction and someone was shooting someone else. Anyone, shooting anyone else.

Yoiks! Maybe Kadaffi *was* paying attention after all. Bill's shorts suddenly headed up, following the antigrav unit. Fortunately, they were the standard trooper industrial-strength undershorts, so Bill was carried along for the ride.

The little white arrow of the commandos lifted gently—and limply—out of the battle. The heavy armor, laden with other military gear and possibly living bodies, slowly rose away from the surface toward the transport.

Bill, on the other hand, was not weighed down at all. He shot into the sky.

The arrow turned and wafted up, pointing the way up to where Captain Kadaffi's bodyguards waited to hose out the suits for re-use. It moved almost delicately, twirling over the battlefield as it gradually rose into the air.

Bill could feel the wind rushing by and hung onto the antigrav unit's straps for dear life as it jerked him back and forth and twisted him around. As rides go, this one was pretty good. He'd paid good money at The Trooper's Friend Amusement Park and Knocking Shop for stuff that wasn't nearly as violent and nauseating. And

they didn't even have the real threat of a hideously painful death, which was a key feature of this one.

It wasn't just the wind. Bill was definitely getting
colder. He whipped up through the clouds, and little
crystals of ice started collecting on all the uncovered
parts of his body. They formed up real nice on his foot,
especially. The frost formed a pattern there, and the cold
started working its way up his leg. The thinner air made
it harder to breathe, and that provided a distraction of
sorts, but wondering which of the two problems would
kill him wasn't much of an improvement over worrying
about just one of them.

His teeth started chattering. His whole body was shivering, and he was sweating with fear. The droplets of
sweat froze up almost immediately, and the shivering
shook them off. Bill was leaving a little delicate trail of
ice particles behind him, shimmering in reflected sun-
light. Which would have been quite pretty—if he'd had
the leisure to reflect . . . and if he hadn't been quickly
freezing to death.

He rolled up into a ball to conserve warmth. He
would've taken his foot off to run the laser over his
hands and body, but he was shaking too much.

There was no screaming this time. Even if he'd been
zooming upwards in the no-moaning section, he would
have ignored it now. Moaning was all he had left, and
he was determined to enjoy it to the fullest. Moaning
was something of an art form in the troopers, and troopers were expected to stay in practice, in case of just such
an emergency. It was closely related to screaming, so a
lot of what Bill moaned on the way *up* was very similar
to what he had screamed on the way *down*. He even did
them in the same order. He started with a few rounds
of "Oh bowb, oh bowb," moved on to "Please don't
let me die," segued into "Heeeeelp," and finished up
with the old standard, "Mommy!"

It did about as much good as the screaming had, which

is to say none at all. But it was important to do these things properly. Freezing and asphyxiating to death while flying straight up into the stratosphere in his underwear hadn't been covered in boot camp, nor in Bill's fusetender's specialist course, nor had anyone ever mentioned the possibility any time since then. So he had to rely on his carefully honed instincts, but moaning definitely seemed to be in order.

Bill couldn't think what should come *after* the moaning, so he ran through it again, and then got ready to lose consciousness. He had a lot of experience at that.

He could see the stars now, not twinkling very much because the air was so thin up here. He was definitely dying. He could tell because both his feet felt the same now, the manufactured one and the real one, and the force of the wind past his ears was diminishing. His nose was numb, and his hands weren't far from it. And now he was hallucinating.

There was no question he was hallucinating, because he was seeing a huge black shape looming over him, and here he was on the edge of space, where there sure weren't any huge black things. And he was heading straight for it.

The big black thing grew eyes, opened them, and stared straight at Bill. A terrible glowing red mouth opened. Then the monster sprouted arms, lots of them, and started to reach out to gather Bill into its hideous stomach.

Bill wanted to go out kicking and screaming, but there wasn't enough air left to scream. He activated the knife in the bottom of his foot. The saw popped out instead, and he attacked with that.

There was a solid *k-thunk*. Somewhere in the distance Bill thought he could hear something screaming. There was one flash of light, and then everything went black.

*CHAPTER* **3**

FLAT. GRAY. COLD.

Bill gradually became aware that the whole universe was flat, gray, and cold. At least, what he could see of it.

Was this heaven? Bill didn't have a very clear idea of what heaven was supposed to look like, his early religious training being only a dim memory, but this didn't seem quite right.

On the other hand, Bill had considerable experience with waking up someplace he didn't recognize without knowing how he'd gotten there. This seemed a lot more like something repulsive, as always, rather than heaven.

He took a closer look at his new surroundings. Flat, really flat, and pretty boring. The surface had a regular texture to it, a sort of a raised herringbone pattern. That somehow looked familiar.

Where had Bill seen it before? In an astronomy textbook? No, he'd never seen an astronomy textbook. In an old issue of *Imperial Geographic*? No, Bill only looked at the pictures in the ads of the naked women in that. In a training manual?

That rang a bell. It wasn't in a manual, but it had something to do with the military, didn't it?

Yes! It was skid-proof metal decking, just like the floor in the barracks. Bill's spirits rose immediately. Maybe none of this was real—maybe he had never been volunteered into the commandos and gone on that mission, maybe he had just fallen down and hit his head on the way out for his twelve-hour pass, or fallen down drunk after coming back in. That was something much more familiar and reassuring.

Then Bill remembered something about a giant black monster with lots of arms and legs, and the hair on his neck lifted in horror at the thought. A spider? It had to be a dream. There were no spiders in space, and he'd never heard of a spider that big, nor had he ever seen one on any of the planets whose hazards he had suffered during his years of service. Not even Veneria had spiders *that* big. He must have been dreaming about spiders.

That was a little unusual. Most of Bill's alcoholically inspired dreams involved giant snakes and rabbit holes, or elephants trying to pull peanuts out of caves, or sometimes even Bill doing with women all those things he never got the chance to do when he was awake. Sometimes he would dream about barrels of beer, vats of vodka, showers of champagne, waves of whiskey, and all the other alliterative intoxicants that life in the Troopers made so necessary. But he never dreamt about spiders.

Then what could this all mean—?

Bill lifted his head off the decking and looked around. The room didn't look much like the barracks back at Camp Buboe. It looked a lot like a loading dock, or a warehouse, or a troop transport.

A troop transport? Bill let his head fall back to the floor with a thud. Had he fallen back into the clutches of the heroic Captain Kadaffi? The spider would have been better.

Bill gazed dully across the clean, freshly painted metal deck. The wave of despair at the thought of being a survivor and a hero in the commandos kept him from realizing at first that the deck was *too* clean, too freshly painted. The personnel hold of a troop scow would never be this clean. Why, they were even built dirtier than this.

So just what the bowb had happened?

Bill finally realized that the only way to find out anything was to get off the floor and look around.

He stood up. The helmet of his combat jump suit was lying to one side, next to the antigrav unit. He was wearing only his shirt and his uniform undershorts. So he hadn't imagined all of that, after all. That was interesting.

He was in a small room that could have been anywhere, as long as that anywhere was in the Troopers. The walls were the same color as the floor, and the same material. If it had been meant for carrying enlisted men, the walls would have been the most nauseating greenish yellow imaginable. If it were for officers, the walls would have been papered in red and gold flock. So he was in a cargo bay. The only thing to do, then, was explore.

Except that the one door was locked. Bill pounded on it for a while, and at last a voice came from the other side, saying, "Yeah, yeah, keep your bowby pants on."

"I haven't got any pants," Bill whined.

"Then hold your horses," the voice instructed.

"I haven't got any horses," Bill lamented. "I used to have a robo-mule, but that was a long, long time ago, on a planet far, far, away, when life was much better and I was studying to be a Fertilizer Technician." He sobbed sympathetically at the happy memory.

"Just shut up and wait for the General," the voice explained.

"Tell me you didn't just say 'General,'" Bill hoped.

"OK. I didn't just say 'General,'" the voice agreed. "But here he comes."

The heavy metal door flew open, catching Bill square on the temple. He stumbled, staggered, and fell to his hands and knees.

"Well, well, well. What have we got here?"

Bill looked up at the voice. It was invisible, of course, but its owner was about the size and shape of a refrigerator box. He had more stars and ribbons on his chest than most refrigerator boxes (except, of course, for the emperor's own refrigerator box, which held ministerial rank). The name 'Weissearse' was embroidered in gold thread over the breast pocket of his desert camouflage muumuu.

"That isn't necessary, Trooper. A simple salute is sufficient," the General alliterated.

Two MPs hauled Bill to his feet, where he snapped off his classiest two–right–handed salute. Normally, this was Bill's best shot at impressing an officer, but General Weissearse was having none of it. "Let's have a little chat," he said. "Escort this Trooper to the debriefing room."

The MPs picked Bill up by the elbows, tilted him sideways, and carried him out into the corridor. A few turns and hatchways later, with only a few severe blows to the cranium getting through the tight spaces, Bill was being strapped into the debriefing chair. A debriefing technician taped electrodes to Bill's skull and genitals, and another used what appeared to be a small machete to take a cell sample.

The General hulked in one corner muttering to himself. Bill could hear him, but if he turned to look, the electrodes kicked in with a blast of voltage, The more he turned, the more sizzling the electrodes became. Staring straight ahead proved to be a much better idea.

"So, Trooper," General Weissearse smarmed cordially, "how long have you been a spy for the Chingers?"

"Not very long, sir." Bill jumped as the technicians gave him a little shot. "I mean of course I'm not a spy at all. Death to all Chingers! Look in my record—the only Chinger I ever saw alive was one I met in boot camp." He twitched again. "I hate all Chingers!" This time they didn't give him a jolt, so he got bolder. "Could someone tell me where I am?"

"Don't you know, Trooper? Weren't you sent here by the Chingers to worm your way into our confidence and sabotage our plans?"

"Look at my helmet! It's Imperial issue, standard stuff!" Bill yelped, anticipating his next shot of electricity. "Look at my underwear!"

"Don't be disgusting, Trooper."

"No, really, I'm as loyal as any Trooper!"

The General snorted. "So you admit being disloyal?"

"Yow!" Bill jerked from the jolt. "No, no! I love the Emperor! I love the Empress! I love all the Emperor's sisters and his cousins and his aunts! His sisters and his cousins and his aunts!"

General Weissearse turned to one of the technicians. "Raise the voltage. He must be lying, trying the old song ploy." He loomed flabbily over Bill on the table. "You know that there is nothing to be gained by lying—other than my displeasure," he thundered. "The Lord will bring the truth to light in the end!"

"Would that be Ahura Mazda?" Bill asked.

"God is on our side!" roared the man in the muumuu. "It is only right that we help him out with a few electrodes. Besides, it's better that you suffer a little here and come to the truth than that you suffer the eternal pains of damnation later. Right?"

"Of course, sir. Right. Only the truth?" Bill smiled broadly and falsely. "You let me know what it is, I'll say it, and everybody's satisfied? OK? Yeow!" he yeowed as a blast of current fried him.

"Wrong answer, Trooper. You don't understand." Weissearse shook his head sadly and his jowls joggled. "You must unburden yourself of the truth freely, without prompting or duress. Raise the voltage again. Jolt him if he lies. Report, Trooper!"

Bill looked around for help. A couple of bored technicians were standing, scratching their crotches as they took in all the excitement. One was at the electric controls that were frying Bill. The other was staring at a screen and waiting for the computer to spew out its response to Bill's tissue sample. They started talking quietly—which involved more crotch scratching—about their plans for the evening, which weren't much since they were stuck on a small ship in the middle of nowhere. All of which did not help Bill in the slightest. This was a situation that called for daring, creativity, and imagination. Unfortunately, Bill was completely devoid of all three qualities. "Yeow!" He was also running out of time.

As quickly as he could, he cobbled something together out of the most recent literature he could remember reading. He knew that Generals generally liked complicated stories, so he worked out a story involving three brothers named Karamazov, a desert planet with gigantic worms, a Japanese prince named Genji, a robot detective who looked like a man, and a great white whale. He wasn't sure where the whale came from, but the rest were from recent issues of *Superlative Six Superhero Comix*.

But General Weissearse was destined never to hear this epic tale of military logic and excuse-making. Just as Bill began—"Call me Bill"—the computer chimed and began to print out a long, long scroll of paper.

"Aha!" The General pounced, and was reading before the paper had finished coming out of the wall slot. "Your real name is Bill, isn't it?"

"I just said that, didn't I?"

"There's no use denying it. Your DNA doesn't lie. I

know who you are. I have your complete service record here, *Bill*. And a pretty darned impressive record it is, too. 974 citations for drinking on duty. 63 promotions, including a field commission. 62 demotions. Aren't you embarrassed to wear the uniform of the Imperial Space Troopers?"

"Yes, you're right, I am," Bill sobbed. "Expel me from the corps. I am not worthy."

"It's not *that* easy, Trooper. Let's see. You have a fusetender's rating. Your last assignment—I'm impressed. You volunteered for the commandos."

"I was proud to do it for my Emperor and my General, my General," Bill fawned. "Yeow!"

"Knock off that voltage!" the General ordered the electroshock technician. "It looks like you're the only survivor of your mission. One survivor—a tremendous success. I'm impressed, which is pretty darned rare. You're the first Trooper in four years who has survived one of Captain Cadaver's missions. That shows initiative. Or luck. Or the fact that you are a Chinger spy."

He read further down the list, and stopped in shock. "Praise the Lord!" His eyes glowed as he looked at Bill. "God is on our side!" the General enthused. "Working in mysterious ways his wonders to perform. And working only on *our* side because all Chingers are dirty atheists!

"You, Bill, are the answer to my prayers!"

Bill looked around. He didn't get any electrical shocks, but he didn't get any enlightenment, either. "What prayers? What answer?"

"Untie this man!" Weissearse ordered. "This Trooper is a galactic hero!"

"That's me all right," Bill said as he was helped to his feet. "Bill, the Galactic Hero. You can look on the cover if you don't believe it."

"No need to do that," the General said, "it's all right here in his service record. This man was decorated by the Emperor himself! He wasn't even trained as a gunner, but in great and terrible battle against the Chingers he saved his ship, the great *Christing Keeler*, mistress of the Imperial fleet. Defeat was imminent, disaster was at hand, the very fate of civilization as we know it hung in the balance, but he shot down the last of the vile Chinger attackers. Without training!

"It can only have been the very hand of God in action!"

Embarrassed by the novelty of kind words Bill scuffed his Swiss Army Foot on the floor. "Maybe, but really— it was just a lucky shot."

"There is no luck," Weissearse thundered. "Only the divine and mysterious intervention of the Lord Himself can possibly have been responsible for this! Bill, here, must be one of those protected by God's divine love? And he has been sent to us for a purpose!

"Get him some pants."

Half an hour later Bill found himself in a fresh uniform, sipping fresh water and trying to pretend it was vodka, and listening to General Weissearse and trying to pretend that the General made any kind of sense at all.

"Do you have any questions, Trooper Bill?"

"Questions?" Bill frowned with unaccustomed thought. "Once maybe. This ship looked just like a space spider when I bumped into that. I never saw a ship like that before. Was that a dream?"

The General chuckled benevolently. "No, Bill. I had this scout ship designed to look like a space spider, so it would be harder for the enemy to find us."

"But there are no such things as space spiders," Bill protested.

"Precisely," the General explained. "So there is nothing designed to detect them, and we are perfectly safe. The Lord helps those who help themselves, after all.

"And it is important that this ship be safe, now that I have been entrusted with this great mission. Now we will be even safer, with you, God's own tail-gunner, protecting us and watching over us. Our vile and insidious foe will never penetrate our defenses with you, Bill, God's chosen vessel, in our crew."

Bill was certainly flattered to be considered God's chosen vessel and all that, but he wasn't too sure what god this screwball General Weissearse meant. It probably wasn't his own god, Ahura-Mazda—Bill had been raised as a strict Reformed Zoroastrian—and it may not have been the official god of the official Imperial Religion, which was of course the Emperor himself, but that still left a lot of possibilities. In an empire as big as the Empire, there were a lot of religions and nut-cults operating alongside the official one.

Besides the Reformed Zoroastrians, there were the Revived and Amplified Mithraists and the Acoustic Mithraists, the Sunnis and the Moonies, the Buddhists and the Twiggists and the Leafists, worshipers of the Sun and Tau Ceti and Aldebaran and NGC4681, Confusionists, Taoists and Jonesists, Voodoos and Hindus, Elvists and Lennonists and Marxists (with a different sect for each of the brothers except Zeppo and Karl, who shared one), and enough other groups that the non-denominational chapels on a large ship were kept going around the clock with services.

So there was no way of telling what god General Weissearse knew was on his side, and Bill figured it didn't matter all that much, but he would like to know which one had chosen him. If he was going to offer up a prayer, it would be nice to know the proper address. On the other hand, the General might just be screwball and talking through his hat.

Bill hated to do it, but he had to find out more. He forced himself to take another sip of the—gack!—water, and asked, "That's all very flattering, sir, but what the bowb are you talking about?"

The General stood up and started pacing. "I like your face, Bill, if not your manner of speech. You have maybe gotten into some trouble with drinking before, boyish kind of prank. But that won't happen on *this* ship." Bill nodded his agreement reluctantly, unseen by the general who ignored him, getting his jollies instead from inside inspiration.

"I trust you. The Lord tells me to trust you, so I do. We have a good relationship, the Lord and I.

"But that's not what I want to talk to you about now. We have been honored with a very special mission. You and I—well, mainly I, with some help from God and you—will strike a blow that will preserve truth, justice and the Imperial way of life. To us the great privilege has fallen, and to us the glory of victory will come."

Bill was too old a Trooper to be taken in by the inspiration bowb. "This mission, sir, it doesn't by any chance involve people shooting at us? I've had some bad experiences with that . . ."

"Not at all," Weissearse heartily reassured Bill. "This will be a simple surgical strike, with very little resistance. The enemy is wily and dangerous, but we will destroy all their guns in the first wave, so we will be perfectly safe. There is nothing to worry about. Nothing can go wrong. Trust me."

# CHAPTER 4

AS GENERAL WEISSEARSE DESCRIBED THIS wonderful mission, on which Bill would become a hero at absolutely no risk to himself, Bill became possessed of the feeling that not only wasn't this kosher but that there was a very big pig in the poke. He was sure that the eye-rollingly religious General was full of bowb. There was nothing he could put his finger on—or wanted to—but the more certain Weissearse got, the more doubts Bill had.

At first look it appeared to be as straightforward a piece of stupid military-political action as the Troopers ever got sent into. The enemy was the government of Eyerack, a planet in rebellion against the Emperor. General Weissearse was very clear that neither he nor the Emperor nor anyone else in the entire military establishment had anything against the people of Eyerack. It was only the government, and even then only a very small group of the top leaders of the government, who would be bombed into submission. Of course, it was inevitable that some small number of those who had taken up arms against their loving Emperor might be accidentally blown to smithereens, but in modern total warfare a small number of casualties—say, five or ten—could not be helped.

Had this been an ordinary planet in rebellion, the normal practice would have been to blow it up. Careful studies had been done at the Runt Corporation, the Emperor's favorite think tank, about the different possible ways of removing the cancer of rebellion from the body politic. Blockade was no good; it took a long time, there were no dramatic opportunities for press conferences and briefings in front of colorful maps, and pictures of the action wouldn't even make the back pages of the newscomix without an order from the Imperial Office of Freedom of the Press. Negotiation was even worse; it had all the faults of blockade, plus it showed weakness, since only weaklings talked first and shot later. Sometimes the Fleet would negotiate after a battle, but only if they could find a few prisoners, something that happened quite rarely. Only blowing up a rebellious planet provided a quick and guaranteed solution, as well as pictures that deserved front-page coverage. It was right there in the officers' manual—"If a planet rebels against the Emperor, blow it up."

But Eyerack was different. Eyerack had something that no other planet in the galaxy had. Eyerack had a neutron mine.

Neutrons, as everyone knows, are very, very small. They are so small, in fact, that you could walk right past one on the street and never see it. And they aren't very sociable, so you don't often find more than a hundred or so together. But you need a great many neutrons to make a neutron bomb.

Of all the weapons humanity had ever invented, the absolute favorite of all the Generals and admirals and field marshals was the neutron bomb. It blew up real good, made a pretty picture that kept the Emperor happy, killed all the enemy soldiers (and sometimes some friendly ones, although that was a minor point), and *left all the hardware unharmed*.

What could be better?

So Eyerack was very important. Without the Eyerackian neutron mines, there could be no more neutron bombs. And if Eyerack was blown up, it would be very hard to find the mines. They might even be lost forever.

But for the time being the Empire couldn't have any neutrons anyway, because of this rebellion thing.

Somehow, someone had made a terrible mistake. The entire Office of Neutron Procurement had been drafted, court-martialled, and shot for not paying enough attention. While they had been napping, Eyerack had held free elections.

This, by itself, would have been enough to cause a crisis throughout the halls of power. Free elections had been banned centuries ago, under the Edict for the Preservation of Freedom and Democracy. But it was even worse than that.

If free elections were not bad enough, the Eyerackians had overwhelmingly voted for peace.

The only use for neutrons was in making neutron bombs—for killing people.

*No more neutron exports!* was the cry of the peace party. No more war!

For the empire, there was only one possible response.

A nice, clean, quick, precise, deadly attack. A surgical strike, cutting out the bad and leaving the good. With maybe every one on the other side killed so there would be no worry about any future problems. The Empire needed those neutron mines back but quick, and in working order so the Chinger War could be continued and expanded. So what it needed at once if not sooner, was ruthless dedication and an officer who would stop at nothing. Other than peace. It called for General Weissearse. Now General Weissearse was calling for Bill.

"Yes, Bill, the Lord hath provideth thee in my hour

of need! And with thy divinely guided hand on my tail gun, we cannot faileth!''

Bill gave up on trying to explain to the General that he didn't know how to operate a tail gun. Why bother? What he really needed was to keep his ass covered and find whoever on this ship was running the illicit still. Someone always was. And the tail gunner's turret would be an ideal place to hide a few bottles; no one in his right mind would go there if he didn't have to.

He groveled his way out of the General's cabin. Bill wasn't sure that the General even noticed; he was busy in some kind of religious-military ecstasy.

Since the General's ship, the *Heavenly Peace*, wasn't a normal flagship, but a scout, it didn't have the normal accouterments of combat command. The General's cabin took up less than a full deck, for example, and didn't even have the standard private gym; the General had to use the same one as the other officers, and share the steam bath and masseuse. The ship was so small that there was only one dining hall, for the officers, and one mess hall for the enlisted men which was really the engine room with tables over the pipes. It got so hot that most Troopers couldn't eat; which was OK since the food was inedible in the first place. The chef in the dining hall would have access to the wine cellar, of course, so he wouldn't bother with a still. Bill went to visit the mess-hall cook.

He steered his way through the rows of dented metal tables and pipes. The tables had carefully been arranged in a pattern about halfway between zigzag and random, so the troopers had to keep their eyes down and their wits about them in order to get across the room without slicing up their knees and ankles. Fortunately, the place was empty—breakfast was just over, and most of the crew was on line at sick call—so he could walk on the tables for some of the more complicated parts.

"Closed. Bowb off," the cook growled.

"And a good morning to you as well," Bill placated.

"Would there be a cup of something dark and hot for a new member of the crew?"

The cook grabbed a cup and dipped it into the sink where a KP robot was washing pots. "Here."

Bill swallowed hard, then took a sip of the liquid. "Yummies!" he lied. "That's *much* better than the pseudo-coffee at Camp Buboe!" He drained the cup, grinned, and held it out to the cook. "Please, sir, may I have some more?"

The cook frowned and glared and grumbled, but he took the cup and dipped it again. This time he tasted it himself.

"You know, you're right. This *is* better than the usual stuff. And cheaper, too. With the money I save, maybe I'll be able to buy Mom that wooden leg."

"Aww." Bill had once had a Mom too, and maybe even still did. The mail didn't get through too regularly, so he couldn't be sure. "Your mom lost a leg? That's too bad. I could recommend a place that's real good for feet, though." He hoisted the Swiss Army Foot up onto the counter.

"No, no, she's got all her parts. She just collects artificial limbs." The cook took a closer look. "That's a real nice foot, I must say. You wouldn't be willing to part with it by any chance?"

"Sorry. It's the only one I've got with me. I could give you the address of the mailorder . . ."

"Well that would be real fine. Now you've done me two favors, and I haven't even introduced myself. Julius Child, Mess Sergeant."

"Bill, fusetender first class and God's own tail gunner."

"God's own tail gunner? Then you've already met the General. What can I do for you, Bill?"

Bill looked around slyly and lowered his voice. "You wouldn't know where I could get some alcohol, would you?"

Sergeant Child looked thoughtful. "Hmmm." He

looked at the racks and cupboards over the stoves and sinks as though he was going through an inventory in his mind. "There's the wood alcohol they use to clean the torpedo tubes, but that'll kill you, and besides, they lace it with saltpeter." He thought some more. "There's the chaplain's sacramental wine, but he's an officer, and officers don't share, and the lock to the wine cabinet is kept in a cage with the chaplain's sacramental rattlesnakes. I think that's out." He looked at Bill for confirmation.

Bill weighed the matter carefully: on the one hand, wine; on the other, virtually certain death. After some time, he reluctantly agreed with Child.

While the mess sergeant was thinking some more, Bill interrupted him. "Surely you could do something? Some leftover vegetables, a little sugar, yeast, water, heat, and if you want to get fancy, a distillation coil?" Bill was no chemistry whiz, but over the years he had picked up a few basic survival skills.

Child looked shocked. Bill knew that look well, having been severely shocked not long ago himself, and looked around for loose wiring. He didn't find any, so he looked back at the mess sergeant, who said, "*Moi*? Make illicit alcohol? Never. I would never consider such an idea. It would violate all my dearest principles. 'Lips that touch liquor shall never touch mine,' so forget about kissing me, too." He would have gone on in this vein for some time if not for the arrival of a trooper in a full dress desert camouflage apron, bearing two buckets of potato peelings.

"Got yer makings here, Sarge. Want me to dump 'em right in the still?"

"Still?" Bill trilled, thrilled. "You *have* got a still!"

"No, no," the sergeant demurred, signaling to the aproned trooper to keep his mouth shut or certain death awaited. "He said *swill*, didn't you, Brownknows? We're having swill for lunch today, made with genuine vegetable peelings from the officers' dining room. It's a big favorite with the men. Bill, you can tell the General that all the troopers love their swill. Yes, indeed."

"Why would I tell the General?"

Brownknows snickered as he put down the buckets. Bill glowered at him. Brownknows glowered back.

The ritual completed, Bill asked again, "Why should I tell the General?"

"You *are* his spy, aren't you?" Child insisted.

"Bowb no!" Bill denied.

"Come on," Brownknows cajoled, "you must be. Most of us on the *Heavenly Peace* are spies of some sort," he admitted.

"And if you aren't a spy for the Chingers," the sergeant reasoned, "you must be a spy for General Weissearse."

Brownknows nodded agreement. "Yeah. You haven't contacted any of the other spy cells on board. The only person you've spent any time with is the General. And if he thought you were a Chinger spy, you'd be dead. And you're not. Therefore, you're his spy."

Bill considered this deeply, and analyzed his priorities and loyalties. "If I *were* a spy for the Chingers," he offered, "and I'm not saying that I am, mind you, just say if I was would I be able to get a drink then?"

"Well," Child conceded, "on the basis of your being a Chinger spy I would have no objection to finding you a drink—of which there isn't any on the ship because our beloved General has forbidden it to enlisted men. But then, if you were working for the Chingers, then Brownknows here would have to arrest you, because he is a spy for the Imperial Office of Anti-subversive Activities. Isn't that right?"

"Not exactly," Brownknows corrected. "My assignment here is to spy on the officers, not on the enlisted men. I also steal scraps from the dining hall for the still that we would have if the General permitted it. But there's nothing in my orders about Chingers or Chinger spies. Or enlisted men, for that matter. What about you?"

"I have nothing to do with Chingers," the Mess Sergeant demurred. "I'm spying for the Society for the Preservation of Ancient Morality. SPAM has been infiltrating mess halls for centuries, restraining the natural hedonistic tendencies of troopers and making sure that they don't get overstimulated by their food.

"On the side," he continued, "I get a stipend from the Desert Monsoon Foundation for not serving any Eyerackian delicacies, which might undermine the morale of our troops.

"But," Child insisted, "none of this has anything to do with you, Bill, because you have already denied being a Chinger spy."

"Exactly," Bill claimed. "Isn't that what I would do if I really was a Chinger spy?"

"Possibly," Brownknows waffled.

"But not necessarily," Child refuted.

Bill wanted to continue the argument, but he couldn't think of any more synonyms for "said." Instead he wandered off to find the tail gun and see if an earlier tail gunner had left a bottle behind.

Word spread rapidly on the *Heavenly Peace*. None of the other crew he saw wanted to talk to him, not even to tell him where to go, or, for that matter, where the tail gun was. They wouldn't even talk to him when he offered them hot sauce from his combat foot.

On the other hand, that left him with few distractions, and within a couple of hours he was snugly fitted into the tail gunner's bubble turret.

Bill had seen something like this before, but only once, and a long time ago. In fact, the last time was what had gotten him here, the time that made him a galactic hero. Since he'd been heroic and wounded and on the verge of passing out, and was never any too bright to start with, his memory of the gun turret on the *Christing Keeler* was pretty hazy. There had been a joystick with a red button on it, and a screen with red and green lights, and no instructions.

This one was much more elaborate. The sides of the turret were all covered with garish paintings of Chingers and tanks and bridges exploding under a banner reading, "Nintari Electronics Presents: TAIL GUNNER!" The chair swiveled around and tilted back and forth. Instead of a joystick there was a yoke, like the controls for a hovercar, and it had two buttons, one red and the other black. The black one had a little label that said **STRAFE**. The red one had a little label that said **BOMB**.

When Bill strapped himself into the seat, the screen lit up with a full-color computer-animated portrait of the Emperor, eyes wandering gaily and separately about. After a minute that picture was replaced with one of General Weissearse in his desert camouflage muu-muu. This picture said "What's your name, Trooper?"

Bill said, "Bill."

Across the bottom of the screen scrolled TROOPER BIL.

"No," Bill said. "Two L's." But the screen ignored him.

"You are a new gunner, TROOPER BILL," said the animated General. "Do you want a training session?"

"Sure," said Bill.

The screen ignored him again. "Press the red button for live fire, or the black button for training," it said.

Bill thumbed the black button.

"Deposit a coin now," directed the computerized Weissearse. A digital clock materialized beside him and started ticking down from ten seconds.

With combat-trained reflexes, Bill reached down to the coin dispenser in his Swiss Army Foot and pulled out a quarter-credit coin. As he expected, the slot was just below the screen. He got the coin in with four seconds to spare.

A list of targets and point values lit up the screen, with a picture of each type of target. They ranged from one point for a single enemy soldier up to a million points for a little man with black hair, a bushy moustache, and a very bad complexion. The little man was labeled **ENEMY LEADER. EXTRA TIME AT 500,000 POINTS** scrolled across the bottom.

Somewhere, as though from a great distance (although nothing here was more than six feet away), Bill thought he heard a choir singing "The Trooper's Hymn," but he shook his head and it went away.

The image of General Weissearse returned, holding a pointer and standing in front of a chart. "The black button, marked STRAFE, will destroy little things." He indicated pictures of a soldier, a tent, and a tank, and each one blew up in turn. "The red button, marked BOMB, will blow up big things." He pointed to pictures of a bridge, a building, and a battleship, and again each one blew up. "There is one exception." The ENEMY LEADER appeared on the chart. "You must use the BOMB to get the points for the ENEMY LEADER. Otherwise it looks as though you were trying to kill him, and you get no points.

"Press the black button when you are ready to begin."

Fortunately for Bill, there was a change machine in the gun turret. When he ran out of quarters, he could get more without having to leave the turret, and have the amount deducted directly from his pay. Since he couldn't get a drink and no one wanted to talk to him, he spent the rest of the trip to Eyerack trying to get his name into the TAIL GUNNER! Hall of Fame.

# CHAPTER 5

IN SOME WAYS THIS WAS THE BEST DUTY
Bill had ever pulled. People left him alone, he had nothing to do but play video games all day long, and no one was trying to kill him. On the other hand, he was sober all of the time, and there was nothing even remotely female on board the *Heavenly Peace*, not even the ship's cat—an evil-looking tomcat with only one eye and ears scarred and torn by the spacerats that it hunted through the bilges. But at least for the moment no one was trying to kill him, which made up for a lot.

General Weissearse showed up in a live broadcast to the gun turret a few times, and Bill had to listen to the man pray and preach, but even that was tolerable once Bill realized he didn't have to stay awake for any of it. And the general kept saying, until Bill believed it, that this would be a safe battle. He wouldn't even have to attack any people, only guns and buildings that wouldn't fight back.

Bill did kind of regret that he couldn't get all of a million points for ENEMY LEADER, because in the

Live Fire mode a million points was exactly what you had to get to win a twelve-hour pass. But he also had learned from the game that ENEMY LEADER types were usually surrounded by other types carrying guns and missiles and weapons of all sorts. And these types got offended if you tried to kill their leader. By and large, Bill had gone out of his way for years to avoid offending people with lots of weapons.

So when the real General interrupted the computer-animated general to tell Bill that they were in orbit around Eyerack, and had been so for two weeks hoping that the Eyerackians would see the error of their ways, Bill didn't immediately start pleading for his life. He didn't even try to remember any of his boyhood prayers. He just wondered if he could afford enough quarters to finish the battle.

He squandered one of them in the second slot he'd found under the screen. The chair tilted back and started to vibrate, and in an instant Bill was asleep.

He dreamt of home, of his mother and his robo-mule and the great house with the white columns in front, of the cheerful midgets who came to play and sing in the yard as he marched down the road, paved in yellow brick, that led to the recruiting office. Somewhere deep in his subconscious he knew that the farm hadn't been anything like that, but it had been so long that he wasn't really sure any more.

Then he dreamt of his kindly old school mistress, Ms. Phlogiston, who had helped him to start taking his correspondence courses in Technical Fertilizer Operation, courses that he would now never finish. She told him, in his dream, "You must always be ready, Bill, to take advantage of whatever opportunities present themselves. And in order to do that, you must plan carefully. Every great venture must have a plan, you know." But why was Ms. Phlogiston wearing a muumuu? And why was she yelling at Bill?

"Bill! Bill! Hallelujah, son, it's time to wake up!"

It gradually came to Bill that it wasn't Ms. Phlogiston yelling at him, it was General Weissearse. Reflexively, his eyes popped open and his two right hands saluted. "Yes sir! Yes sir! Three bags full, sir!"

"Praise the Lord, son! No, no, that's not an order. But wake up, Bill, we're about to go into glorious battle against the godless heathen who are threatening the very basis of our civilization, who are attempting to undermine the moral and religious principles that are the core of the Empire and of all humanity, who are an embodiment of evil unknown since the days of fabled Earth itself . . ."

Bill's eyes started to close again.

" . . . destroy the enemy in our midst in order to destroy the atheistic Chingers . . ."

His eyes closed fully, and his breathing got deeper and steadier.

" . . . the glories of heaven to our victorious troops . . ."

The next thing Bill knew, the general was shouting at him again through the video screen.

"Wake up, Bill! As I was saying, only through your eternal vigilance, and the Lord's hand on your guidance and targeting computer, can we save the galaxy from atheistic totalitarianism."

Automatically, Bill said, "Yes, sir," but he did wonder idly how atheistic totalitarianism differed from being in the Space Troopers. Probably had fewer chaplains. But of course, the Chingers and the Eyerackians didn't believe in the Emperor, the hand of whose own, personal, stand-in Bill had once slobbered over, when he was getting his medal that certified him as an official Galactic Hero. That kind of personal contact tended to reinforce a naive farm boy's loyalty, and Bill had always been intensely loyal to the Emperor, even if he couldn't quite remember the Emperor's name.

While Bill was thinking about all this, General Weissearse finished his pep talk. "So, Tail Gunner Bill, are you ready to go?"

"Yes, sir. I've been practicing for weeks."

"Excellent! Remember, we're not actually going to be killing any people in this attack, because all human life is sacred, even that of godless traitors who deserve to be tortured to death. Just blow up the buildings that are marked in red on your screen.

"And here's a little something to show my confidence in you. We attack in five minutes. The Lord, the Emperor, and I are all counting on you. Good luck and God bless!"

The general disappeared from the video display before Bill could react. Bill was more interested in what was happening at the change machine anyway. Coins were pouring out of it, and its display was blinking **NO CHARGE! NO CHARGE! NO CHARGE!** Five credits worth of quarters! Bill wiped away a tear at this sign of his commander's faith in him.

He gathered the fallen coins and stacked them neatly on the little shelf above the controls. The first coin went into the slot, and for the first time Bill pressed the red button for live fire.

The target screen wasn't the same as the one he'd been training on, but that was fine. Bill had learned to expect surprises in combat.

The *Heavenly Peace*'s artificial gravity held everything steady, but Bill's chair swiveled and swooped and twisted so he could get fully nauseated by the dive through the atmosphere toward the Eyerackian defenses.

There! A small dot on the screen glowed red! All that time and all those quarters spent in training were not wasted. Bill waited until he was in range, then launched a smart missile.

They were called smart missiles, but in fact they were even dumber as Bill himself, which was pretty dumb. It wasn't enough to show them the target; Bill had to steer them in to the target by the TV pictures they sent back from their nose cameras. The experience was very much like a roller coaster ride in which you got blown up at the end, or like being a commando, except that you didn't actually die.

There were explosions all around, but Bill ignored them. He concentrated on guiding his missile straight into the gun emplacement. At the last second, he could see the Eyerackian gunners running away from their posts, and then the screen went blank. At the top, it said **GUN EMPLACEMENT: 50 POINTS**, and the score total went to 50, and then there was another dot of red set up for him.

The great battle had begun.

# CHAPTER 6

IT WAS NOT THE MOTHER OF ALL BATTLES. But at least it was the second cousin, twice removed, of all battles.

The *Heavenly Peace* was the scout and command ship for the great assault, and teeniest vessel in the armada. The General's ship had barely enough firepower to destroy a planet. But it led the greatest armed force ever assembled since the last one, in February. Millions of heroic troopers aboard thousands of gallant ships displayed their heroism by dropping bombs from a very great distance. And behind all this great venture lay a single only partially unhinged mind, the dominating intelligence of General Wormwood Weissearse.

The Emperor had said, "Go, thou, and return unto me my straying sheep of Eyerack," and the General had leaped into action with a brilliant plan, glazed eyeballs and organizational genius.

Well, that wasn't *exactly* how it happened. It was really like one aide whispered the news from Eyerack into one of the Emperor's ears, the ear that was slightly less deaf, and the Emperor mumbled something and drooled significantly, and another aide, stationed a safe distance from the Imperial mouth, announced the Emperor's inspirational words and thoughts. The General's plan boiled down to "bomb 'em back to the Early Stone Age." And his organization consisted of saying to a bunch of officers, "Get your ships and come with me."

But the roboflacks on board the *Heavenly Peace* got their story into circulation and kept it there, and the citizens of the Empire, who knew little and cared less, figured that it must be true. There were even those very few who were dim enough to believe the endless flow of military propaganda.

So it was that the great fleet swooped down on the defense installations of Eyerack in wave after wave, in a massive surgical strike that would wipe out the entire defensive system of a planet without killing any civilians and maybe no more than 2.5 defenders. It was almost too good to believe.

But believe it people did, particularly Bill. He could see the evidence with his own eyes, right up there on the video screen—and video screens don't lie, do they? He was seeing the action first-hand, through the nose cameras of the smart missiles that were doing the work. The smart missiles that he, Bill, feeling he was soon to be a galactic hero twice over, was guiding with more than superhuman precision to their destinies.

The first wave of ships, with Bill in the tail of the lead, concentrated on Anti-Spaceship defenses. The vast armada swooped deep into the atmosphere of Eyerack and destroyed whatever weapons down there might hurt them. Thousands of gallant gunners like Bill risked the terrors of modern long-distance warfare—motion sickness, boredom, exhaustion, thirst, horniness—to protect their comrades from the terrible wrath of Eyerack.

One target after another popped red on Bill's screen, one missile after another was launched from the rectal tubes of the General's space spider. Bill's confidence in himself and his weapons systems—they were much too sophisticated to be mere weapons—grew with each direct hit. His first smart missile had hit the gun at which he'd aimed it, but soon he was trying for even greater precision. Now he was putting his missile right down the barrel of a gun, or swooping around from behind into the ammunition stores. And every time, as he had been told, the warning sirens of the incoming missile gave the gun crews time to get the bowb out of there.

Bill started to get giddy with his success. He sent his missiles into loop-de-loops and barrel rolls and Immelmanns, spelled out words with their tracks; he was really beginning to enjoy himself. After a while he even realized that he could use the nose cameras on his missiles to look around the battlefield at no danger to himself.

There was some danger to the missiles, of course. The Eyerackians, not realizing that the huge military force surrounding their planet had nothing but their best interests at heart, were doing their best to shoot down everything in the sky. They would try to shoot down the missiles, and sometimes they would even succeed. Bill hated that, because he needed to rack up as many points as possible. To get extra time so he wouldn't have to add any of his own quarters to the pile General Weissearse had given him. Sometimes the Eyerackian gunners would be shooting at something else, something Bill couldn't see on his screen. And sometimes, Bill started to notice, the soldiers at the guns didn't have any chance to run away when they didn't shoot down the missiles.

The nose cameras blew up with the missile, of course, so he never saw the explosions, but it gradually dawned on him that some of the Eyerackian soldiers were being blown up at the same time. Bill had been partially blown up a few times himself, and he felt a certain sympathy for the Eyerackians.

During a brief slow spell, he took one of his missiles on a little tour of the area. For the first time he could see the whole fleet, spread out across the sky like a patient etherized on a table. There were thousands of ships, ranging in size from scouts like the *Heavenly Peace* all the way up to dreadnoughts that were so big they couldn't come into the atmosphere. The smaller ships were attacking in waves, each wave led by a scout ship, holding them all in neat formations by remote control. Each of the larger ships released its own wave of bombers and fighters and flying missile platforms.

The missile platforms floated high up, over the action, lobbing missiles down through the clouds. The bombers charged straight in at their targets, surrounded by a buzzing sphere of fighters. As Bill watched, a group of fighters detached itself from one cloud and zoomed down to meet another group coming up from below. They were all dots from this distance, so he couldn't tell who was winning, but then a bomber exploded. Bill drove his missile down toward the airfield, which flashed red—**AIRFIELD: 100 POINTS** —just before he hit it.

This wasn't fair! Here the Empire was doing its very best not to kill anyone, and these vile Eyerackians were trying to kill Bill's buddies! In the back of his mind, Bill realized that he didn't really know any of those people, and that, after all, in the Troopers it was always bowb-your-buddy week. Also maybe the weeks of subliminal patriotic music had had an effect on him. Maybe even some of General Weissearse's sermons had sunk in while he was asleep. Maybe it even had something to do with the hypno-coils embedded in the chair. For whatever reason, now Bill was fighting mad.

Now he had a clear sense of mission. His job was to destroy anything that might harm his buddies, his pals, his comrades in arms. And, not incidentally, himself.

He knocked out another Anti-Space-Ship missile base, then obliterated an Anti-Aircraft-Artillery emplacement, then blew up an ammo dump, and destroyed some more AAA, and cratered an airfield, and kicked some more ASS.

By now the Eyerackian defense command had alerted their troops, and the front of the attack wave was itself being attacked. Bill couldn't concentrate only on ground installations any more; he was using his lasers now to pick off missiles that were aimed at *him*! His chair was swooping and dodging and ducking and spinning and bobbing and weaving until Bill was glad the only food he'd had in weeks was the liquid nutrient gruel from the dispenser in the turret. Anything else would be all over his video screen.

There were no more slow periods. Bill was too busy shooting down attacking fighters and missiles, most of the time, to worry about where they were coming from. All he knew was that they kept coming. The only breaks he got were when he had to put in another quarter, and he couldn't risk taking very long with that. Fortunately, he was racking up enough points to keep the guns going for a long time.

Bill barely had time to think about how safe the General had promised this mission would be.

Now that he was mostly using the lasers, he had a sort of normal view to the rear. It was punctuated by arrows and flashing red signals and green halos around the ships of the armada, but it still showed him what was going on. And what was going on was that all hell was breaking loose.

The entire battle was being fought in the air, and it was moving around the planet at great speed. But it was still a battle.

Missiles were flying up toward the ships and down toward the ground and between the ships and the bombers and fighters of the fleet and the Eyerackian fighters. Laser beams crisscrossed the sky, burning or exploding or slicing up whatever they found. Sometimes a laser blast from one of the Imperial ships would slice open one of their own bombers while trying to intercept a fighter. Without the red and green markings on the screen, Bill would never have been able to tell what side anyone was on, and he sure hoped that the other attackers had a system like his. Even with it, sometimes his screen was just a big mass of red and green dots.

The sky was full of whizzing death. The *Heavenly Peace*, being in the lead of the attack, only had to worry about what was actually being aimed at her—although that was quite enough, thanks. The rest of the ships and planes were flying through a steady rain of shells and missiles and bullets and fighters and bombers and electronic chaff and debris. Mostly debris. The ships had repeller fields to take care of the smaller pieces of metal, but the planes were getting chewed up by left over chunks of bombs and missiles and shells and even other planes, chunks that were just as good as a bomb or a laser in tearing off a wing or plowing through a cockpit or a gun turret.

There was no way to tell anymore who was shooting whom. If a bomber—or, sometimes, an Imperial ship—went down, it might have been from Eyerackian fire, or Imperial fire, or just from running into junk.

It didn't matter any more. Bill wasn't paying attention to selected targets any more, either. Not even to his point totals (which were pretty low, because flying debris, no matter how dangerous, wasn't worth any points at all to the computer). He just shot everything that looked like it might be getting close to him.

And then suddenly everything was getting farther away.

It took a couple of minutes for Bill to realize that the *Heavenly Peace* had pulled out of the attack, back towards a planetary orbit. While his turret computer worked out his total score and bonuses for the day, General Weissearse popped up in a little mortise in the upper left-hand corner of the screen.

The General had put a belt around his muumuu so it looked more like a standard uniform, although not much. He was standing in front of a hologlobe of Eye-rack that had arrows and diagrams all over it, and an off-screen voice was saying, ". . . your favorite General and mine, troopers and journalists, here he is, Stormy Wormy Weissearse!"

There was a burst of applause from the recorded studio audience.

"Thank you, thank you," the General said. "As you know, our purely defensive and completely justified and morally pure attack on the godless heathens of Eyerack began just a few hours ago. All the operational details of the attack are, of course, absolutely secret and will remain so forever. But I can give you some idea of how the operation is going so far.

"Everything is just hunky-dory."

The screen went to a split screen. On the right was a shot of the reporters, who were jumping up and down like school kids, waving their arms and trying to get the General's attention, despite being on a different ship a million miles away. A trooper slipped a microphone in front of one of them and handed her a slip of paper.

"General Weissearse," she read, "to what do you attribute the overwhelming success of today's battle?"

"Of course, most of the credit has to go to me, as the creator of our brilliant strategic plan and leader of our gallant troops. And I suppose a weensy bit of it has to go to those brave men and women who are putting their lives on the line in this daring, yet completely safe, operation. But most of all, our victory is due to our faith in God, and God's faith in us as his instrument in chastising the atheistic warmongering rebels of Eyerack. All of our success is owed to the Lord. Hallelujah!"

Bill thought that maybe a little of the success was owed to all that practice he'd put in on the way here, but this news conference was a one-way broadcast.

Another reporter had been given a question to ask. "Were any of our brave warriors injured in the great battle?"

Bill was particularly interested in this one, since he had himself incurred a small blister on his trigger finger, and hoped for a Purple Kidney (the traditional medal for blisters, scratches, bruises, and paper cuts received in combat, and usually reserved for officers).

"I'm glad you asked me that," General Weissearse began. "As you know, there are millions of troopers involved in this great venture, and in any exercise of this magnitude a certain number of losses is inevitable. Every injured trooper is a tragedy, of course, and my personal staff will be sending my personal computerized form letter to the personal families of every trooper with a Class C-7 injury (Yucky Flesh Wound) or higher.

"Fortunately, it looks like we won't be writing any of those letters tonight."

Bill breathed a big sigh of relief. From what he'd seen, there was a strong possibility that some troopers might have been injured as high as Class A-2 (Completely Dead, No Parts Reusable; the only higher class, A-1, Complete Vaporization, was considered the same as Absent Without Leave, and was a court-martial offense). When a ship blew up in the atmosphere, as a bunch of them had, people were likely to be seriously injured after falling five or ten miles to the ground. Bill wasn't sure how this hadn't happened, but he was glad no one had been hurt badly.

The trooper with the microphone handed over another sheet of paper.

"What sort of punishment has been meted out to the disloyal and godless enemy?"

"Much less than they deserve," the General said. "Of course, we can have no detailed figures on enemy casualties, but we have utterly destroyed the Eyerackian Triple-A and have wiped out the ASS. Our intelligence reports tell me that there is so far only one confirmed Eyerackian fatality. This was an old man who was visiting his son's missile base as the attack began. The surprise and fury of our attack were too much for the old man, and his heart stopped. Even though we were not directly responsible for his death, I have sent a message of apology to his family.

"Now that the Eyerackian defenses have been obliterated, in the coming days we will concentrate our attacks on the factories where these vile people have been producing weapons of mass destruction such as we, ourselves, would never use. We will also be targeting the military facilities that support those factories, supplying them with raw materials, parts, electricity, food, and sewage treatment. And we will do this without inconveniencing the civilian population in any way."

Bill was amazed for a moment at the precision of his own video-controlled weapons systems, and even so he had a little trouble with the idea of bombing sewage plants and blowing up only the sewage from arms factories. But the subsonics and the hypno-coil kicked in, and the moment of doubt quickly passed.

The computer finally finished computing Bill's scores. They were pretty good, if you included the bonuses for not getting killed, but not enough to get into the top ten. They certainly weren't high enough to get that twelve-hour pass. Bill might have minded that more if there'd been somewhere to go on a pass, but on this ship there were no women, and the only places to go were the enlisted men's lounge and the mess hall. Since no one in either place would talk to him or give him a drink, he wasn't missing very much.

This was in any case much more interesting than the General's press conference. Bill was busily figuring out how many more points he could get if he didn't have anyone shooting at him when the General stuck his head into the turret.

Bill saluted with both hands and tried to get to his feet. He'd been sitting in that chair for a couple of weeks, though, and couldn't quite manage it. He fell back into his accustomed position, with the video screen before him. General Weissearse was taking another question from a reporter.

Bill looked back toward the door. General Weissearse was standing there, looking impatient and vaguely concerned. Bill looked back at the screen. The same General was there, explaining how the eleven seconds of videotape from a nose camera that they were about to see was absolutely typical of the millions of missiles fired.

"It's a miracle!" Bill screamed, and tried to fall to his knees.

*CHAPTER* **7**

ONCE THE GENERAL HAD LOOSENED BILL'S
seat belt and slapped his face a few times to get his
breathing started again, he explained.

"Only the Lord can perform a true miracle, son.
That's just videotape. I recorded it this morning, before
the attack."

Bill tried again to prostrate himself, and got caught
again by the seat belt. This time he pulled himself up.
"Ahura-Mazda must have imbued you with his spirit,
to give you information about the future like that! It's
a miracle!"

General Weissearse looked impatiently down at Bill
and considered explaining, then sighed. It didn't look
as though it would do much good, not to this moron,
so he let it be. "Okay, son, it's a miracle, isn't the time
to talk theology.

"I just wanted to make sure you're all right, and get
you ready for tomorrow's battle. We're in for a tough
one, and I'm counting on you."

Bill looked up at his video screen once more, and back

at the general. "But—but—" he butted. He shook his head to clear it. "You just said that we destroyed all the enemy defenses."

On the screen the general was explaining again how much he and the emperor regretted this entire unpleasantness, and how they both hoped that no one else would have to die because of it.

Here in the turret he said something else. "You did a great job today, Bill. I bet you didn't even use up all the quarters I gave you, did you?"

Bill pointed with pride at the two coins on his shelf.

"Good. You'll have a chance to use them soon. Now you'd better get a good night's sleep. We're going in again in the morning, and you're going to be busy. There are going to be a lot of people shooting at this ship, and it's up to you to protect me. Remember the great honor I've given you, and keep my interest in mind, and you'll be all right."

General Weissearse walked to the door. "Oh, yes. And you got a medal. Get it from the machine."

The little one-line electronic display on the change machine was now blinking between **GET CHANGE HERE** and **CREDIT: 1 MEDAL**. Bill pressed the credit button, and the line switched to **DEPOSIT ONE QUARTER OR TOKEN**. This would leave him with only one for tomorrow's battle, unless he wanted to shell out some of his own hard-earned credits. Although he had nothing else to spend them on, and if he died tomorrow they wouldn't do him any good anyway, he did kind of resent having to pay the Emperor. He wasn't surprised any more, but he did resent it, just as a matter of routine.

Bill already had a medal or two stashed somewhere in his gear, and was entitled to wear the treasured Purple Dart with Coalsack Nebula (although he'd lost the actual medal long ago); but he finally decided that an extra decoration on his uniform could only make him more attractive to the Trooper groupies he kept reading about but never seemed to meet. If he ever did meet one, the extra quarter-credit investment would be well worth while. So he put half his stash back into the machine.

A terrible grinding noise came from the machine's innards. It moaned and cried and creaked and squealed, giving Bill a nostalgic thrill. It reminded him of his time as a drill instructor. A low rumble began deep inside the change machine, and moved slowly toward the dispenser. With a bounce and a clink, something fell into the little bin.

Bill fished it out. On one side of the oval, metal object was a portrait of the Emperor. It looked a lot like the portrait on all the coins, except it had been stretched diagonally. Around the rim ran the Imperial motto, IN HOC SEOR WENCES, also looking as though it had been stretched at an odd angle—the same odd angle, in fact. On the other side Bill could dimly make out what had once been an elegant sculpted bas-relief of the imperial log cabin where, by tradition, all emperors were born. That image, so familiar from all those quarters, had been mostly flattened out, though, and the words "Operation Friendly Persuasion Combat Medal" stamped in. A small hole had been punched in one end.

It wasn't the fanciest piece of jewelry Bill had ever seen. In fact, it reminded him very much of a souvenir he had once made out of a capper centicredit coin at a carnival. He wondered if he still had that souvenir; if he did, he could hang the penny and the quarter together, and they would make a much more impressive display. The chances of anyone looking closely enough to read the inscription on the penny—"I survived the Phigerinadon IV Fertilizer Fair"—were pretty slim.

Of course, the chances of Bill's recovering any of his treasured possessions, including his foot locker, were just as slim. Only victory would allow Bill to return to the relative safety of Camp Buboe, and there might very well be a court-martial waiting for him there. Failure to die on a suicide mission might get you a commendation, but it was also a violation of a direct order. Sad to say, Bill's safest refuge for the time being seemed to be right here in the rear turret of the *Heavenly Peace*.

It would be stretching the truth to say that Bill awoke refreshed. He did awaken, though, and that was enough of a triumph for the moment. He'd been sitting in that turret for weeks, on a liquid diet, hooked up to a catheter, mastering the intricacies of the Nintari TAIL GUNNER! system and being utterly ignored by the rest of the crew, so his legs were getting just a little stiff. But waking up after a battle was still better than the alternative.

He didn't awaken gently, either. The klaxon rang right in his ear, and a voice screamed, "Dive! Dive! DIVE!"

Bill jerked spasmodically. His whole body twisted around, except the part that was attached to the catheter. That stayed behind. It hurt enough to bring him to full consciousness.

The video screen was flashing in all the colors available to neon. DEPOSIT COIN OR TOKEN NOW! DEPOSIT COIN OR TOKEN NOW! I REALLY MEAN IT! YOU BETTER GET THAT COIN IN RIGHT NOW! NO KID-DING! DEPOSIT COIN OR TOKEN NOW, OR GET READY TO DIE!

Bill grabbed his last quarter and slammed it into the slot. He ran through the menus into combat mode as fast as he could, and started looking for targets.

All he could see was sky and spaceships, none of them highlighted in red. Then the view swung around as the *Heavenly Peace* came out of her dive and went on the attack.

The ground lit up in the bright orange of rocket exhausts, and a moment later it was a patchwork of red, if the enemy triple-A had been wiped out, they must have rebuilt pretty fast. In the background, Bill heard a clatter of quarters as the change machine anticipated his needs. He wasn't going to have much time to ask for coins today.

The Eyerackian defenses started out behind the first wave again, as they had the day before. Bill got busy picking off missiles that were aimed at some of the ships trailing the spider-shaped scout. But the defenders got organized faster today, and concentrated more of their effort on the leader.

A group of Eyerackian fighter planes drove up just behind the *Heavenly Peace*, not attacking her directly but trying to cut the general off from the rest of the wave. With help from the gunners on the other ships, Bill sliced them to ribbons with his lasers.

A big target flashed on his screen: AMMUNITION DE-POT, the screen said, 1000 POINTS. Bill needed to rack up points today if he wanted to get that 12-hour pass. The smart missile was launched even before his lips worked their way through the message.

Eyerackian lasers stabbed out at the missile, trying to keep it from its goal. Which would keep Bill on this ship longer than necessary. He started to take this war personally. He made the missile swoop and dive, turn and twist, weaving it through the web of defenses toward the little bull's-eye that the computer painted on the entry door. Compared to gunning down the counterattack, this was almost fun.

Bill corkscrewed the missile in around a laser beam. He looped it around an anti-missile missile. He ducked it under some exploding flak, and bobbed it over a line of bullets. He swung it around an oncoming fighter and swerved past an office building. He jumped it over a hedge and threaded it through a copse of trees. And then there was nothing but a straight run for the door.

There was a sign on the door, and he focused on that as the missile rode in to the ammo dump. There were no pictures, so it was hard to read, but he worked his way through all the text just an instant before the bomb hit it dead center.

AIR-RAID SHELTER—MAXIMUM CAPACITY 600 CIVILIANS was what it said.

Something seemed wrong to Bill.

Hadn't General Weissearse said something about not killing any civilians? It stuck with him because it had seemed a little odd at the time; normally the idea was to kill as many civilians as possible, and it wasn't the military way to make a change of this sort, or to give up the chance to kill people who wouldn't be fighting back.

It didn't seem like a *bad* idea, not killing civilians, just an unusual one. Bill could even vaguely remember being a civilian, and at the time he had thought not being killed was a really good idea. And now it looked very much like he had just killed up to 600 civilians.

But the video screen had clearly labeled the building an ammo dump.

Moral dilemmas were not within Bill's limited expertise. He wasn't at all prepared to deal with this one. He bucked it upstairs.

The general responded to Bill's call by appearing in the same small box on the screen where the press conference had been. He was watching another video screen and cheering the bombs as they dropped.

"What can I do for you, Bill?"

"General, Sir, I think I just blew up a civilian air-raid shelter!"

"So?"

"Well, aren't we supposed to be avoiding that?"

"Sure we are, Bill, but don't worry about it." General Weissearse waved the issue away. "It must be a mistake of some sort."

"But my target computer gave me 1000 points for it, just like an ammo dump!"

"Then it must have been something else, like an ammo dump." The general gave a small cheer as something blew up on the screen before him. "What made you think it was an air-raid shelter?"

Bill thought hard for a second. "There was a big sign on it that said 'Air-Raid Shelter.'"

General Weissearse laughed the hearty laugh he had learned at the Imperial Military Heroes Academy. "That's just enemy propaganda, son. Pay it no mind." He looked intently at the screen for a moment. "Now you'd better do something about that fighter closing in on us, or we'll both be in heaven tonight."

The long hours catheterized in the chair paid off. Bill sliced up the fighter and touched his laser to the heads of a small flight of incoming missiles.

The morning dragged on. Even the adrenaline rush of combat can get routine if there is never a break to recover, and the action continued without a pause. When he was not under attack, Bill had more ground targets than he could possibly hit. And he was under attack most of the time.

It was tense. It was exhausting. It was mind-boggling. But it wasn't interesting.

It only became interesting a little after lunchtime.

Bill had gotten adept at picking off single incoming planes or Missiles. Two at a time was no longer a challenge. Three at a time was enough to require some concentration. Four at a time was beginning to get difficult. Above five, and he needed help from the nose gunner on the ship behind the *Heavenly Peace*. At this precise moment, there were five manned fighters and six missiles highlighted in red on Bill's screen.

Bill fired a heat-seeking missile into the pack and hoped for the best. A smart missile caught a fighter, just as the heat-seeker took a missile. Bill switched to the lasers. He swept them through the incoming pack and blew up three more, plus one of his own escort fighters. The gunner on the ship behind got two fighters before he developed more pressing concerns of his own.

Another heat-seeking missile blew up another fighter. Bill fired yet another before he knew what the first had done. Then he switched back to the lasers and touched off a missile before it could reach him. The last heat-seeking missile caught the last fighter.

Nailing ten incoming targets at once was pretty good. Bill knew it was a personal best, and thought it might be a record of some sort.

Unfortunately, it wasn't quite good enough. Bill had intercepted ten, but there had been eleven, and that last missile found one of the small and vulnerable spots on the *Heavenly Peace*.

There was a great explosion and the ship went into a steep dive. Alarms went off, even more of them and louder than reveille. The safety harness and the catheter tightened up, cutting off Bill's breathing and nearly cutting off small but important pieces of his body. His video display went solid red. Electric blue letters flashed, **PREPARE TO DIE! PREPARE TO DIE! PREPARE TO DIE! WE'RE GOING DOWN! PREPARE TO DIE!**

A small window—the one that Bill had started to think of as the general's private window—opened in the screen. "I'd like to thank the whole crew for all your effort in our great endeavor. I'd particularly like to thank you for making me look so good. I only wish it were possible now, in the moment of your greatest trial, for me to be with you. However, the *Heavenly Peace* has been shot down, and I am much too important to the war effort to be captured or killed.

"So I am leaving in my command pod. But I wish you every success in getting to the surface alive. If you are captured, which you surely will be if you aren't killed in the crash, please remember that you are expected to die under torture before telling them anything at all. Not that you know anything useful, but it is the principle that is important.

"Remember that you will all be eligible for citations, as long as you die under torture. If you survive, of course, you will be eligible for court martials followed by execution as deserters.

"Good luck, and gods bless."

It was a stirring and touching speech, especially compared to Captain Kadaffi's farewell to the troops.

The music to the well-known hymn, *Nearer, Whichever Deity Applies to Thee*, welled up, and the words scrolled across the bottom of the screen. A beautiful picture of the sky filled the rest of the screen, punctuated by General Weissearse's private cabin–cum–escape-capsule lifting itself to safety.

Once more, Bill prepared to die.

# CHAPTER 8

ALL BILL COULD DO WAS HOLD ON FOR THE
ride.

It was a pretty good ride, if it wasn't going to end
with a crash, with loops and swoops and turns and dives
and an extraordinary variety of bumps and sudden turns.
The pilot managed to find an instant to turn off the
klaxons, but there was no way to shut down the hymns.
So the deadly dive was accompanied all the way down
by pious and mournful music.

Bill tried singing along to the music, but he didn't
know any of the official Imperial non-denominational
hymns. He only remembered one prayer—"Save me! I
don't want to die"—and his repertoire of assorted
screams for mercy and pleas for help was getting stale
from overuse. All those responses to dire crisis that had
proven so effective in the past were meaningless now.

Even though the safety belts were holding him in his
seat so tightly that he could move only his face and his
toes and his fingers, he was still holding on to the straps
as though his life depended on it.

What his life really depended on, of course, was the skill of the pilot of the *Heavenly Peace* and a great deal of luck. The pilot was doing what he could, and so far the luck was holding. For one thing, none of the other Imperial ships were shooting at them, and Bill knew for certain that that had to be pure luck. For another thing, none of the Eyerackian gunners seemed to be aiming at them; this might have been luck, or maybe the ship was swerving around too much for them to hit. Or maybe the Eyerackians didn't think it was worth shooting down twice.

That didn't mean that bombs and missiles and bullets weren't zooming all around them. They were, and some of them were exploding not terribly far away. On the video screen, over the pious lyrics and the bouncing ball, Bill was getting a close-up view of the death and destruction behind the scout ship. There was some consolation in the vision of the debris and completely exploded ships that were falling down even faster than the *Heavenly Peace*, with even less chance of survival. But not much.

The *Heavenly Peace* was at least still moving forward some. Most of its motion was generally in the direction of the center of the planet, but not all. Bill hoped that they were going enough forward to make a trench in the ground, but he suspected more of a crater effect. Of course, he couldn't see anything then except the sky.

Until just before the very end, when some trees and a couple of buildings swept up into view along the bottom of the screen, moving at the same speed and in the same direction as Bill's stomach. The ship pulled out of its steepest dive and flew almost level for a good two or three seconds.

Then it hit the ground.

*Crunch!*

The *Heavenly Peace* bounced back into the air.

*Crunch!*

The *Heavenly Peace* slammed into the ground again.

Then it bounced high into the air. The back of the gun turret split open, and the video screen and the change machine went flying out.

*Crunch!*

The next impact broke whatever mechanism was holding all the safety straps secure.

*Crunch!*

On the next bounce Bill went flying out the back of the ship, not quite leaving behind the part of him that was attached to the catheter. The pain from that was enough to distract him from his otherwise incredibly painful impact on the surface of a lake.

*Sploosh!*

The cold water numbed his nether parts enough for Bill to start swimming toward the nearest shore.

It was a good job that he'd kept his arms in trim, working the controls of the Nintari TAIL GUNNER!, because in all that time he hadn't walked a step. His legs were utterly useless; even worse, the Swiss Army Foot weighed him down. Even with all the strength of his arms, by the time he got into the shallow water at the edge of the lake he could never have made it out without the help of two kind strangers.

The strangers each grabbed one of Bill's right arms and lifted. They carried him over to the shore and dangled his legs over the grass. "Ready?" one of them said.

"Ready," said the other.

They let go.

Bill crunched instantly to the ground and looking up he could see his two new friends clearly. They were nice-looking fellows, big and trim (if not quite as big and trim as Bill), very polite (if not quite as polite as Bill), wearing neat, well-pressed uniforms (even neater and better pressed than Bill's).

Bill backed up a bit. Uniforms? He took a second look.

Definitely. Uniforms.

Eyerackian uniforms.

Bill was a prisoner of the ruthless, atheistic enemy.

It was bad enough that he'd survived the crash of the *Heavenly Peace*. That was tantamount to death and disgrace by itself. Now he was doomed to go through unspeakable tortures and die anyway. He moaned pathetically.

"Excuse me, sir?" asked one of the Eyerackians. "Are you ill?"

"Should we summon medical assistance?" asked the other.

Bill perked up. "Nurses?"

"Certainly. Doctors, too, if necessary. Will they be necessary?"

"No!" Bill shook his head vigorously. "No doctors. Just nurses. Lots of nurses!"

"Certainly, sir. And were you alone on your ship, or did you have any comrades? Will they be requiring some assistance as well?" The Eyerackians swiveled Bill around on his butt so he could see the *Heavenly Peace*, or its remains, on the far bank of the lake, flames leaping from the great fissures in its hull. Nothing seemed to be moving except the flames.

Bill thought for a second. For all he knew, the whole rest of the crew could be dead. For all he cared, too. But if these Eyerackians were getting ready to torture him, it could only help if he started to cooperate now. "I don't know."

"I beg your pardon?"

"I mean, I was the tail gunner. I never saw anyone else on the ship. Once I went aboard I never even left the gun turret. That's why I can't walk. So I don't know about the rest of the crew."

"Very well, sir." The Eyerackian turned to his partner. "Snarki, you'd better see to it that an aid crew checks the wreck right away."

Snarki moved a few discreet steps away and spoke into his walkie-talkie.

The first Eyerackian asked Bill, "Do you think you

can make it over to that bench, sir?"

All this politeness was insidious. Bill could feel it draining his morale, moment by moment, making him more vulnerable to the hideously painful tortures that awaited him, no doubt, as soon as these two got him behind closed doors. He remembered what General Weissearse had done to him on board the *Heavenly Peace*; the enemy would surely do worse. But for the time being, he had no choice but to go along.

"Frankly, Trooper, I don't think I can move anywhere right now."

The Eyerackian called to his partner, "Better get some transport for this man, too." Snarki waved to acknowledge. "But I should correct your misapprehension, Sir," he said to Bill.

Bill tensed. He'd never had a misapprehension corrected before, and he just *knew* it was going to hurt.

"We aren't troopers. These are Civil Defense uniforms. That's why we're so polite.

"Our function is to keep people safe during an attack, and help the wounded afterwards. Are you wounded?"

"I don't think so," said Bill. "I just can't walk."

Snarki came back over. "Spinal injury, you think?"

"No," said his partner. "He says he isn't wounded, and there's no blood, no pain."

"That's right," Bill told them. "It's just that I've been strapped into my chair for a month or two. All I need is, let's see—" Bill's brain went into creative overdrive. "—lots of bed rest, physical therapy, massages twice a day, and a quart or two of medicinal alcohol each day." Maybe they would wait until he was fully recovered before starting the torture. There was no harm in asking.

"Say, Bismire?"

"Yes, Snarki?"

"Have you noticed this man's uniform?"

"Yes, I have." Bismire lowered his voice. "It smells rather bad, doesn't it?"

"Not that. Look at the design."

"Oh, yes. Sad, isn't it? It desperately needs a bit of piping on the collar, some gold trim, perhaps. Anything. It completely lacks style."

"Well, that too. But look, Bismire." Snarki pointed to the insignia on Bill's uniform.

"By gum, Snarki, I think you're right." Bismire put his hands on his hips and looked at Bill in an entirely new light. "This man is the enemy."

Bill groaned. Now he was in for it. Now they would start torturing him. It was time to start praying; but to who and with what prayer he wasn't sure.

"Precisely," Snarki said. "The enemy."

"What do we do about that?"

"Do?"

"Yes. He's the enemy. Do we capture him, or something?"

"Oh. I see. Quite right. Have you got the rule book?"

Bismire unsnapped one of the pockets in his right pants leg and pulled out a slim volume of regulations, no larger than a Bible. He riffled through it quickly, then settled down to search the index thoroughly. "Nothing here under 'enemy.' Nothing under 'trooper,' either. Hmm."

*Look under 'torture,'* Bill thought, but he didn't say it aloud.

"Try 'capture'," Snarki suggested.

"Oh, I hardly think so," Bismire said. "We are the Civil Defense, and that would be decidedly uncivil." But he looked anyway. It wasn't there.

Neither were "prisoner," "POW," "interrogate," "third degree," "debriefing," "espionage," "torture," "inmate," "convict," "antagonist," "foeman," "combatant," "Amalekite," or any of the other words that Bismire or Snarki or Bill could think of.

"Well, then," Snarki said, "it looks as though we aren't supposed to capture you."

"So?"

"So we'll just have to see to it that you get good

medical care. You've got to get back on your feet, don't you?"

"Well, on my foot, actually." A sad thought occurred to Bill. "I'm not sure the other one is waterproof." He tried to shake the Swiss Army Foot, but he still had no power over his legs.

Bismire and Snarki bent over Bill's extraordinary foot and examined it carefully. "Hmm," said Bismire.

"Indeed," said Snarki.

"Very interesting," said Bismire.

"Indeed," said Snarki.

"Is that a weapon?" asked Bismire.

Bill wasn't about to risk the two Eyerackians' finding a rule in their book that said they had to take away his foot. "No, no, it's perfectly harmless. Sentimental value, mostly, although I do walk kind of funny without it."

"From what we see, you don't walk at all," Snarki mused. "Look, there seem to be little compartments. I wonder what they hold."

Snarki was just about to try to open the Poison Knife Blade slot, and Bill was getting ready to try to lunge with the upper part of his body at the lower part of it, when the ambulance wailed up beside them.

Two orderlies in Civil Defense uniforms pulled a stretcher out of the back. Two men in similar uniforms, but with gold braid, got out of the front.

Bill's crest fell. No nurses. He turned to Bismire. "No nurses?"

"Apparently not. We did request them specifically, didn't we, Snarki?"

"Yes, indeed, Bismire. But there's a war on, you know."

"There certainly is, Snarki. And you know, Trooper, your bombing campaign is causing a lot of casualties, so nurses are in particularly short supply right now. But don't worry—these are two of our very best doctors. Let me introduce you to them."

"You might want to get his name, Bismire, so you can do that."

"Excellent idea, Snarki. What is your name, Trooper?"

"Bill," Bill billed. "With two L's."

"Ah," said Bismire. "So that isn't just an accent. And what is your proper title?"

Bill's permanent rating was as a Fusetender First Class, but it had been a long time since he had tended any fuses; even longer since he had done it when he was supposed to. So he took full advantage of the exalted, if temporary, status he had achieved at Camp Buboe. "Brevet Lance Corporal," he claimed.

"My, my, that does sound impressive," said Snarki.

"Well then," Bismire said, "may I introduce Dr. John Watson, Brevet Lance Corporal Bill; Corporal Bill, Dr. Watson. Dr. Walter Huson, Brevet Lance Corporal Bill; Corporal Bill, Dr. Watson. Dr. Huson, I believe you already know Snarki. Snarki, Dr. Watson. Dr. Huson, Snarki. Snarki, Dr. Watson."

Bismire was just getting into introducing the orderlies all around when Bill interrupted.

"Isn't this something like a medical emergency? I think I should be taken to a nurse right away."

The very Civil Defense team looked at Bill doubtfully for a moment, then at each other. In unison, they shrugged.

"Very well," Bismire said. He seemed to take charge of the situation. "A preliminary diagnostic examination is in order. As a matter of routine, we will get a second opinion. That is the proper way to handle the matter, I believe. Is that how your own people would do it?"

Bill decided not to tell the Eyerackians that his own people would have been torturing him by now, just to find out if he knew anything useful. They would probably get to that soon enough, without his encouragement. "Absolutely," he said.

Bismire thought for a moment. "Both doctors will

examine you right here, Watson first, Huson second."

"Who?" Bill asked.

"Watson first."

"What?"

"Huson second."

Snarki scratched his head. "I don't know."

"Third base," Bill said.

"I beg your pardon?" Bismire asked.

"That just popped into my head," Bill explained. "Does it mean something?"

The Eyerackians conferred. At last Dr. Watson proclaimed, "Possible head injury. Now let's look at those legs."

# CHAPTER 9

DESPITE HIS SITUATION, BILL COULDN'T help but feel a certain glow of patriotic pride.

If this was the best effort the Eyerackians could muster, they wouldn't stand a chance against the Imperial Troopers.

If this hospital was a fair example of their war effort, they might as well surrender right now.

Bill looked around. There was only one other bed in his room, and the civilian assigned to it was free to come and go as he pleased. The man was out wandering the halls now, when he should have been (as Bill knew from experience) lying there, moaning in pain, hoping that the surgeons had, in fact, taken out his appendix and not something more interesting and/or vital.

The walls of the room were clean and white instead of being a familiar and dirty nauseating mustard yellow.

There were no bars on the windows. Through the glass Bill could see something big and green—an almost perfect hologram of a real, live tree.

There was no loudspeaker built into the pillow for

announcements and reveille. Instead Bill had been awakened by an orderly bringing him breakfast. A meal that had included a number of ersatz items that tasted suspiciously like real food.

Bill had even seen a live, human, female nurse the day before. She was hardly a trooper's dream come true—she bore more than a passing resemblance to Bill's quondam comrade Sergeant Brickwall, except for the teeth—but she was inarguably human and almost certainly female. The playful roundhouse punch she had given him when he pinched her left him some hope of further, more intimate, romantic encounters.

All of this left him with a professional soldier's healthy contempt for civilians who played at war. Even though Bill's dearest dream, beyond even getting a real human foot at the end of his right leg, was to become a civilian himself. But that was more like a fantasy than a realistic ambition.

In the meantime, the Eyerackian military hadn't yet tortured him for what little useful information he might have; they hadn't even sent someone around to interrogate him. This was probably to make him worry—soften him up. And they apparently weren't doing anything to keep him from getting up and walking right out of the hospital.

Of course, the main reason he was in the hospital was his complete inability to walk, but the Imperial military hospital would have had him in chains, just to be sure. This place only had him hooked up to some electrodes that he could rip off any time he pleased.

In fact, Bill thought, things could be worse. Even though he was on a world that was doomed to bitter and total defeat at the hands of General Weissearse and his armada, this was the best vacation he had had since his secret mission against the hippies from Hellworld had begun with a luxury cruise.

If only he could get a beer.

He was just settling in for a little nap—his third since

breakfast and it would just about take him up to lunch-time—when a man in a white coat came into the room. Bill stifled the impulse to salute. Even though the man turned out to be a doctor—his little nameplate read PRESUME, L. I., MD—he was still a civilian.

Dr. Presume checked his clipboard, then the compu-chart hanging at the foot of Bill's bed.

"So, Bill, is it?" He didn't look up or wait for Bill's response. "Can't walk, eh? And you're in the military, I see. Well, we'll have you walking around and marching and shooting and doing all that other soldier stuff in no time. Let's have a look at you." Dr. Presume took a small salt shaker out of his pocket. He made a soft whir-ring noise while he ran the salt shaker up and down, just above Bill's legs. Where the electrodes were at-tached, he sprinkled a few grains of salt.

Bill watched all this intently. "What does that do?" he asked.

"Absolutely nothing," the doctor said. "But it makes some patients feel as though something is happening while I look at them. I got it from an old holovision series."

"So Doc, I guess I'll have to be here for a couple of weeks, maybe months, right?"

"I know how anxious you must be to get back into the action and excitement, Bill. So I'm going to do everything I can to get you back to your unit by to-morrow. Where is your unit?"

"*Tomorrow?*" Bill was aghast. A proper military hos-pital would have taken that long just to figure out what piece of him to cut off.

The doctor looked at him with faint amusement. "Of course tomorrow. You just need some exercise, and the electrodes on your legs are exercising them." He checked a dial. "Right now, you're walking at an easy pace. Tonight, you'll be jogging comfortably. Tomor-row morning, you'll be playing championship football. And all without leaving your bed! By lunch tomorrow,

you'll be able to walk on your own! Isn't science wonderful?"

Bill looked at his legs. They didn't *look* as though they
were walking, but he had learned not to ask too many
questions. They never led to anything good. Answering
them wasn't much better.

"Now, about your unit. Your buddies must be looking for you, but we seem to have lost your records.
Where were you assigned?"

At last it started. Bill knew, now, that he would be
hounded day and night, his legs forced to perform in
increasingly bizarre athletic events—golf, football, team
handball, even synchronized swimming—until he told
the sadistic Dr. Presume everything he knew, and more.
He braced himself for the pain and barked out, "Bill,
Brevet Lance Corporal, serial number 295675
6383204596 8132011245 1231245263121452."

"I beg your pardon?"

"Bill, Brevet Lance Corporal, serial number 295675
6383204596 8132011245 1231245263121452."

Dr. Presume scratched his head. "I didn't think serial
numbers went that high. We don't even have anything
like that many people on the whole planet. Well, let me
take that down, and we'll see if we can track you down.
Could you repeat it once more?" He held up a small
recording device that looked suspiciously like a salt
shaker.

"Bill, Brevet Lance Corporal, serial number 295675
6383204596 8132011245 1231245263121452."

"Very well. We'll see if the computer knows where
you belong. But it would be so much easier if you just
told me, you know."

"Bill, Brevet Lance Corporal, serial number 295675
6383204596 8132011245 1231245263121452. I don't have
to tell you anything but that."

"Am I missing something? You aren't allowed to talk
to doctors? Is this a new rule?"

Bill shook his head tensely. "Not doctors, the enemy.

I don't have to tell the enemy anything but my name, rank, and serial number."

The doctor still lacked enlightenment. "And doctors are the enemy?" Bill shook his head. "Me, I'm the enemy?" Bill nodded, waiting for the pain.

Dr. Presume looked at the chart again. "Nothing here about a head injury. Or a possible nut case," he baffled. "What makes you think I'm the enemy?" Dreams of a published paper glinted behind his eyes.

"Maybe I shouldn't tell you." Bill tried to figure. Was he better off here, where they might send him back to some unit he'd never seen before in an army he didn't belong to? Or should he tell the doctor he was an Imperial Starship Trooper and probably be tortured to death, and if not that then put in a prisoner-of-war camp for the rest of the war? Hmm. Three possibilities: probably dead, probably dead, and probably uncomfortable but probably alive. "I'm an Imperial Trooper, but I don't know anything, so there's no point in torturing me," he said belligerently.

"Oh, that kind of enemy!" Dr. Presume smiled gleefully. "That explains it!" Bill braced himself for the worst as the doctor leaned in close. "All the other residents will be so jealous that I've found you. We knew there was a Trooper here, but the civil defense people didn't fill out the paperwork for you and we didn't know who you were. There's a reward for finding you, and now it's mine!"

"A reward? Like in dead or alive?"

"Sort of. Except it's from ENN, Eyerackian News Network. They want to interview you, and introduce you to our president, Millard Grotsky. You're quite a celebrity, you know." Eyeballs aglow with ambition, Dr. Presume scurried out of the room, planning what he would do with the reward money.

Celebrity, eh? Bill had never tried that one before, but it sounded as though it involved cocktail parties and women, two commodities of which he had limited experience but extravagant fantasies.

He stretched luxuriantly and grabbed the remote control for the holovision set above his bed.

The first show he found was a theological discussion of the true nature of "updoc," the perfect state for which Bugs, the first Neo-Zen Master, had long sought.

*Click.*

A sports announcer wearing a military helmet explained that today's baseball game was being delayed until the live bomb could be cleared from the infield.

*Click.*

The image of a news announcer floated over film of something that might have been an exploded ammo dump. She said something about how it was really a shelter, and that civilians had been killed.

*Click.*

A talk show, featuring women married to men whose mothers were virgins.

*Click.*

An old show about a bunch of people marooned on an uncharted planet and their inept attempts to get rescued. Bill watched this one for a while, until he realized they were never going to get off that planet.

*Click.*

And suddenly the familiar image of General Weissearse floated in the holovision tank before Bill. The general looked a lot more grim than he had in the first press conference. Maybe this one had been taped after the *Heavenly Peace* got shot down, instead of in advance. He was wearing a real uniform now; although the one-piece desert camouflage jump suit wasn't that flattering on a man of his size and shape, it did make him look slightly more serious. This was exactly opposite to the effect of his hat. Bill had never noticed before just how large the general's head was. With all the fatheads among the brass, trooper hat sizes ran all the way up to 9⅜, but General Weissearse's hat was clearly too small for him. It rested politely on top of his head, nestled into his short hair, like the top tier of a wedding cake. Bill recognized that any man who would dress like this in public was genuinely bonkers.

And he was smiling. Bill knew from experience that this man was *really* out of it when he was smiling.

"There is absolutely no truth to this report," he was saying. "All our personnel have been thoroughly briefed on our policy, which is *not* to blow up large numbers of civilians. In fact, they have been warned not to blow up, or shoot, or otherwise maim, wound, or kill *any* civilians at all. So if we blew it up, it was an ammo dump. And if there were civilians in it, we didn't blow it up. It's that simple. The only people who would say otherwise are the godless, atheistic leaders of the poor Eyerackian people, leaders who are trying to cripple the Imperial way of life. We have no quarrel with the people of Eyerack, only with their misguided, evil leader, Millard Grotsky. In fact, if they had different leadership we might just call off the whole operation. Nudge nudge, wink wink."

"General," asked a reporter (and Bill noticed that this time the cards with the questions had been handed out in advance), "does this mean that you are urging the Eyerackian people to rise up in rebellion against the despicable Grotsky?"

"Not at all, nudge nudge, wink wink. Although we do hope that they will choose to return to the loving protection of their emperor. The government of Eyerack is leading its people down the path of perdition and destruction, and is lying to them, as well." He turned and looked directly into the camera. "Your emperor, and we as his servants, would never do such a thing. We are the friends of all humans, and only reluctantly—and as gently as possible—chastise those who require correction." He turned back to the reporters. "And, of course, as we proceed—strictly in our own self-defense, you understand—to obliterate the vast war machine that the madman Grotsky has imposed on the Eyerackian people, it is entirely possible that at some point, through a combination of bad weather, human error, metal fatigue, and the efforts of the Eyerackians themselves, we might accidentally injure an Eyerackian civilian, despite our massive efforts to avoid just that. Should that happen, I want everyone to know that *it's not our fault. It's all Grotsky's fault!*"

Grotsky was evil? He was despicable? He was a madman? Grotsky was the reason Bill was here? A steady rage started to build, until Bill realized that here was the most comfortable he'd been in a very long time.

So Grotsky was an evil, despicable madman. So was every military officer he had ever met. Bill had dealt with worse. Grotsky probably wasn't any worse than, say, Captain Kadaffi. At the worst, Grotsky would want to kill Bill. He didn't like it, but Bill was starting to get used to the idea that almost everyone he knew would try to kill him at some point or another. How bad could Grotsky be?

## CHAPTER 10

THE TWO REPULSIVE GOONS MIGHT HAVE been twins.

They burst into the room with no warning, flinging the door back so hard that it thudded into the wall and all the windows rattled. One stayed in the doorway, blaster at the ready, while the other stomped up to Bill's roommate, glared at him, then rasped quick instructions into his ear. The man trembled as he gathered himself up, pulled himself out of the bed and stumbled from the room.

The goons came toward Bill, menace in their every movement.

They didn't look like the civilians who had been taking care of him for two days. They didn't look like civilians at all, in fact. The blasters were a giveaway, if the uniforms weren't.

Two days of rest, even without recreation, weren't nearly enough to dull Bill's combat skills. Dr. Presume had said that Bill could walk now, but he hadn't tried it yet; this looked like it might be an interesting test.

The goons stationed themselves at either side of Bill's bed.

"This the guy, Sid?" one of them said.

"This is the guy, Sam."

Bill had to look at their mouths to make sure who was speaking. Sid and Sam were both the same height and build, smaller and more compact than Bill but with fully developed muscles. They wore the same uniform, with the same conspicuous lack of the Civil Defense insignia. They had the same close-cropped dark hair, the same trim mustache, the same look of grim determination. Except for being more muscular, they looked a lot like the "enemy leader" icon from the TAIL GUNNER! training game.

But there were only two of them. Two Eyerackians with blasters against one Imperial Trooper who might or might not be able to use his legs. It seemed fair to Bill.

Sid or Sam called out, "Stu! Sheldon!" Two more goons came in. They looked just like the first two. One of the four called out, "Sherman! Steve!" And then there were six.

Could they be clones? Bill had worked with clones before, and hadn't much liked the experience, but he looked carefully at the six men standing around his bed and realized that they weren't quite identical. Someone had picked them very carefully, but there were little differences like the size of the nose and the bushiness of the eyebrows, Bill wondered if they'd really been picked, or maybe put together, sort of like himself. But he didn't get the chance to ask.

"OK, Brevet Lance Corporal Bill, you're coming with us. No questions." Even if they weren't identical, the six men were so much alike that it didn't matter which of them had spoken, and Bill had no idea in any case. It hardly mattered, since these had to be the men from the interrogation and torture division. And even if Bill could handle two of them easily, and four with

difficulty, taking on all six was a surer death than going
with them.

Unless—

Bill swung his legs over, out of the bed and toward
the floor—or toward two of the Eyerackians. As his
right foot came close to the nearest one, he activated the
Poison Knife Blade.

A condom popped out of its slot and skimmed across
the room. The twins, startled, watched its flight.

While they were distracted, Bill activated the built-in
laser in his Swiss Army Foot and swung it around the
room. The end of the tape measure swept out and poked
a couple of the twins, forcing them to back off or risk
a nasty cut.

Bill leaped to his feet and swung out with his fists,
to take out two of the twins in one stroke.

Unfortunately, while the treatments had restored his
legs to their usual strength and muscle tone, they had
also made them very, very tired. Bill collapsed in a heap
on the floor.

One of the twins collected the condom and put it back
in the foot. "You won't be needing this just now," he
said. Another reeled the tape measure back into its slot.
A third went into the corridor and returned (Bill thought
it was the same one, but it could have been yet another
one of them) with a wheelchair.

It took four of them three tries to get Bill off the floor
and arranged neatly, if not comfortably, in the wheelchair. And at last the entire group formed up around
him; one in front, one behind, pushing, and two on each
side.

As they passed through the door and into the corridor
Bill saw that there was a small crowd gathered, doctors
and orderlies and patients and Bill's roommate and even
several nurses. When Bill and his escorts emerged, the
hallway erupted into applause.

Bill cowered into the wheelchair.

The goons stopped and struck poses, basking in the

admiration of their comrades, accepting the glory for (as Bill saw it) subjugating a fearsome and dangerous foe. After a minute or so of heroic basking, one of the twins leaned down to Bill. "You don't want to overdo the aloof thing. The crowd loves to get an acknowledgement from their celebrities."

Bill looked around at the crowd. They weren't screaming for his blood after all. "This is for . . . me?"

"Of course. Give them a little wave and we can get going."

Cautiously, limply, Bill waved one hand.

The noise in the corridor doubled. One doctor fainted and had to be carried away.

Bill blew a kiss.

The noise doubled again. Dr. Presume and the impressive nurse came up and presented a bouquet of roses to Bill.

"I'd like to thank all the little people who made this possible," Bill began.

A twin leaned down. "No speeches. We've got our orders, and we're on a schedule."

Bill waved once more to his fans, and he and his escort sailed down the corridor to a waiting elevator.

"What now?"

"Weren't you briefed?" The speaking twin shook his head ruefully.

"You were supposed to get a full itinerary for today," another twin said.

"You're going to be interviewed on ENN," said another—or maybe the first again.

"But first," said some twin, maybe one who had already spoken and maybe not, "we've set up a photo opportunity."

"You're going to meet our President."

"You mean?" said Bill.

"Yes," all the twins said in unison. "Millard Grotsky himself."

Bill's emotions were in turmoil. Without his ever

knowing it, so much of his life had been shaped by this nefarious Millard Grotsky.

Millard Grotsky had started this war, without which Bill would be—well, actually, he'd be fighting someone else, namely the Chingers. But he was supposed to hate Chingers; hating humans who weren't officers was something new, and hard to learn.

Millard Grotsky had made him a celebrity, which hadn't paid off in any concrete terms just yet but might at any moment. Bill knew about groupies, and had never expected to acquire any, but now they seemed to be almost within his grasp. Metaphorically, anyway. Physically, all that was almost within his grasp was his bodyguards.

Because of Millard Grotsky, Bill had met General Weissearse, who, now that he could do Bill no harm, seemed much less crazy than a lot of officers Bill had known, and a lot more colorful.

Millard Grotsky was still worth a half-million points in TAIL GUNNER!, which would go a long way toward a twelve-hour pass if Bill ever got repatriated.

Millard Grotsky was, according to Bill's friend and mentor (absence and distance *do* make the heart grow fonder, and particularly quickly in one as slow on the uptake as Bill) General Weissearse, the root of all vileness, the most evil man since whoever the last one had been.

Bill was profoundly ambivalent about meeting the President of Eyerack.

All the way over to the Presidential Palace, he wrestled with what was, for him, a deep and complex moral question: Do I take the chance and try to off this guy, or what?

Grotsky had thoughtfully sent over this honor guard to bring him, and that was nice. But he didn't meet Bill at the entrance to the palace, and that wasn't nice. He provided a nifty motorized wheelchair to get Bill through the halls of the palace, and that was nice; but then Grotsky's people wouldn't let Bill race the wheel-chair around, and that wasn't nice.

So Bill was still uncertain what to do when he reached the President's private office, down in the fourteenth subbasement of the palace.

He spun around in the chair a few times while he and his escort and the team of photographers waited for the security checks to be completed, and for the blast-proof doors to open. Then a voice came from inside: "Bill, why don't you come in alone for a moment first, so we can talk?"

Bill knew that this had the potential to be a great moment. As he rolled through the doorway, he knew that he had the opportunity to justify General Weis-searse's faith in him. He could surpass his previous status as a generic galactic hero and become one of the greatest galactic heroes of this year, and maybe last year too!

He was alone in a sealed room with the leader of the enemy. It would be relatively simple to kill Grotsky right there. And that would put an end to the war, right?

His strong right hands twitched with the urge to close around Grotsky's throat. He swiveled around to face the man. His arms reached out—

And encountered something hard and round and cold.

"Would you like a beer, Bill?"

Bill paused only long enough to note that the cap was already off the bottle. After a long swallow he put the empty on the desk, held out his hand again, and said, "Yes, please."

The second beer took the edge off his thirst, and with the third in hand he relaxed and looked around.

The office was tiny, by the standards of the Empire: smaller, even, than an officers' latrine. It lacked the op-ulent decorations of an Imperial office, or latrine, as well. Instead of the classic Old Master paintings, such as *Sad-Eyed Clown*, *Little Girl With Big Round Eyes*, or *Dogs Playing Poker*, the walls were covered with computer screens, holovision tanks tuned to the news channels, and funny-looking rectangular objects that looked like they were made of paper. ("Books," someone explained later. "Like comix, but without pictures.")

Behind the desk was the biggest surprise of all. There sat another of the twins.

Bill blinked.

No, not quite a twin. This man wasn't as imposing as the others; less muscular, not as well groomed, not as good posture. But he definitely looked a lot like the bodyguards.

"You're the despicable Grotsky?"

"Yes," the man said, "I suppose I am."

"You started this war," Bill said sociably, between swigs of beer.

"In a manner of speaking, I suppose so," the madman Grotsky said. "It wasn't really my idea, but, well, yes, I guess I can take the credit."

Bill thought about it. "General Weissearse said that everything was your fault."

"The General is a generous man," the misguided Grotsky said. "Would you like another beer?"

"Sure." Bill sipped and thought some more. "The war wasn't your idea, you say?"

"No, not really." The evil Grotsky leaned forward in his chair and spoke confidingly to Bill. "We're not very good at this war stuff. Not much practice."

Bill tried to reassure the Eyerackian President. "You're not doing badly for beginners. I mean, you've lasted four days now against the military might of the Empire and the genius of Wormwood Weissearse . . ."

"Yes, yes," the despicable Grotsky interrupted. "We get the press briefings live on cable holovision here, too. Actually, I'm not sure who's shooting down more of your ships, you or us."

"Well," Bill explained, "I can't say about any of the other ships, but you guys definitely got the *Heavenly Peace*. That was my ship."

The madman Grotsky brightened. "Really? That *is*

good news. Our own lads shot you down? The *Heavenly Peace*? I remember hearing that name somewhere. Wasn't that the lead ship in the attacks?"

"You bet," Bill said proudly. "The General said I was god's own tail gunner on the ship, even if he never quite explained which god."

"The General?" The misguided and evil Grotsky looked thoughtful. "He wasn't on the ship, by any chance, when we shot it down? Gee, I would so like to meet him, you know. I'm a big fan of Stormy Wormy."

"Really? I never would have guessed. But it's too bad—he was on the ship when it got hit, but his escape pod got away. It was very heroic, for an officer."

"Yes, too bad." The slightly less-despicable Grotsky put another bottle of beer up on the desk to replace the empty one Bill had just put down.

Bill got a bright idea. "Why don't you just surrender? Then you could meet General Weissearse, and the war would be over, and I could go home to Camp Buboe and my foot locker. I really miss my feet."

"I beg your pardon?"

"My feet," Bill explained, lifting the Swiss Army Foot onto Grotsky's desk. "This is the only one I have with me, but I have a whole collection of them back at my base. You wouldn't happen to have any spare right feet lying around in the morgue or something, would you? Much as I like my snap-ons, a real human foot would be nice."

The mildly maladjusted Grotsky started playing with his computer. Bill kept sipping at his beer. Bill made better progress.

"Gee, I'm sorry, Bill, but we haven't had enough people blown apart to have a ready supply of feet. Maybe in a few more days."

"That's OK," Bill said generously. "I'm pretty much used to it by now." But something niggled at the most distant recess of his mind—a recess that was getting more distant with each swig of beer.

"I'll tell you what," Grotsky said, "I'll put you on the priority list for feet. Gee, that's your right foot, isn't it?"

"THAT'S IT!" Bill cried. He looked carefully at his pal Grotsky, checking for seams around the hairline. "You keep saying 'Gee'!"

"Do I?"

"Yes, you do!"

Grotsky thought about it, then nodded. "I guess I do. I must have picked it up from a friend of mine."

"Are you sure?"

"Gee. I mean, yeah, pretty sure."

Bill considered the devious Grotsky. "I used to know someone else who said 'Gee' a lot. My old buddy Eager Beager said 'Gee' all the time." Absence, as they say, makes the heart grow fonder. Bill and all the other troopers had hated Eager Beager with a passion normally reserved only for officers, but the memory of all those boots that Beager shined so beautifully lingered long after the man's smarmy personality had been obliterated. "And Beager turned out to be a Chinger spy." He glared at the misguided and evil Grotsky.

"Well, I'm not a Chinger spy. For one thing, I'm not nearly tall enough. Chingers are seven feet tall, and green, and lizards with tails, and none of those apply to me." Grotsky stood up and turned around. He was right.

Grotsky handed Bill another beer and looked him straight in the eye. "I couldn't be a Chinger spy. I couldn't even *know* a Chinger spy. I'm a real human, after all.

"Trust me."

Bill tried to remember where he'd heard *that* phrase before.

# CHAPTER 11

TWO OF THE BODYGUARDS HELD BILL UP during the photo opportunity with President Grotsky. His legs were pretty much OK by then, but Bill's residual blood alcohol level had gotten quite low by then—down to nothing, really—and that fourteenth beer hit him hard. It was a good thing they had brought the wheelchair.

Bill was essentially unconscious through the trip to the ENN studios, and only slightly conscious through his interview. Fortunately, the reporter was ENN's expert on political and military affairs, so she was used to that. In fact, Bill did a lot better than some of the interviews she'd done before the war.

ENN's Vice President for Patriotic Drum-Beating was so impressed with Bill's on-camera presence—and he was indisputably present, if not coherent—that he ordered the interview shown at least once an hour.

Suddenly, Bill was a star.

The Eyerackians having very little experience with war, and Bill being, as far as they could tell, their only prisoner of war, they had to ask him about the proper treatment of prisoners. He was more than willing to oblige.

"Luxury hotels, usually. With well-stocked bars in the rooms. That part is important. Maid service—yeah, maid service has to be included. *Zoftig* maids. Everybody ought to have a maid. Room service. Real food." Bill drifted off into a reverie of physical pleasures.

"Gee," said Sam or Sid. Now that Bill was a celebrity and a friend of the president, he had two bodyguards assigned to him. "That doesn't sound much like being a prisoner to me. Are you sure about this?"

"Absolutely." Bill nodded his head up and down vigorously. "I've been a prisoner lots of times, and this is how it's supposed to be done. According to the Ginever Convention. Uh-huh, uh-huh. This is it."

Sam looked at Sid, and vice versa. Or the other way around. "I'm not sure we can do that," Sid or Sam said.

"Gee, that sounds awfully expensive," the other one said.

"Besides," the first bodyguard said, "there's your publicity tour. Not every place we're going has a luxury hotel. And most of the good hotels are full of reporters anyway. There aren't many rooms left."

"Well," Bill said, "you wouldn't want it to get back to the Empire that you're mistreating prisoners. Then they'd really get teed off at you."

Sid and Sam looked at each other. "You mean they're doing this to us without being mad at us?"

"Not *really* mad."

"Uh-oh," Sam and Sid said in unison.

Bill's first stop was at a supermarket. There was a little platform set up, and the local mayor made a speech and introduced Bill, and then Bill lifted up his Swiss Army Foot and sliced through a big red ribbon with his laser torch. The crowd went wild.

Bill was a little surprised that the supermarket was

underground, but his mother had taught him to be polite and not to ask too many peculiar questions when he was a guest.

Next they went to a mall, where Bill signed autographs and had his picture taken with local politicians, damp babies, and suchlike.

It wasn't quite what Bill had in mind when he thought of celebrity—he wasn't surrounded by hordes of pneumatic young women begging to warm his bed—but it wasn't too bad. He got fed regularly, and it was almost real food, not something that had been recycled and reconstituted. He got to sleep in a real bed without being in a hospital and in momentary danger of death. He had his good buddies Sam and Sid to hang around with, and they never tried to kill him even once (which was more than he could say of any of his other friends since joining the troopers).

People treated him in a very odd way, too, besides not trying to kill him. They called him "sir," and said "thank you" when he signed his eight-by-ten glossy for them, even when he spelled their names wrong, and they asked him to do things instead of ordering him to in a loud voice.

It was very peculiar, but Bill was afraid to ask about it because then it might turn out to be a mistake, and he liked it.

At his third stop, where he got to introduce the latest models of hovercars at the auto show, he came up with his brilliant idea.

The models who were demonstrating the latest models all wanted his autograph, of course. They were the first in line, in fact, because they had to get back to work standing next to the cars and pointing roughly in the direction of the theoretically new and incredibly desirable features.

Sam or Sid held Bill down in his seat and pushed a picture in front of him. Sid or Sam put a pen in Bill's hand.

"And what's your name, dear?" Sam or Sid asked the first model. They had learned very quickly just how bad an idea it was to let Bill talk to attractive women in public; the first time a good-looking girl asked for his autograph he had grabbed her and it took five minutes to pry him loose.

It didn't really fit the image President Grotsky wanted Bill to project. Since then the S-men had limited Bill's communication with such women to signing his name.

The statuesque redhead said, "Kitty."

Sid or Sam leaned down to whisper in Bill's ear so he could spell the name correctly. "For my good friend _____ , Fight the good fight!" was already stamped on each glossy, in a fair imitation of Bill's handwriting, so he just had to fill in two names, and he already knew how to spell his own. But Bill was smarter than they thought: he could get most of the standard four-letter names on his own, and many of the five-letter ones. So he was already writing when the bodyguard said, "Big k, little i, little t, little i."

And when he handed over the picture, with a big smile and a bigger wink, he had finished writing not only the two names, but also, under his autograph, "Room 318," which he had carefully memorized when they checked into the hotel. By the crowds gathered to see him then, he figured Kitty and the other models would have no trouble figuring out which hotel it was.

And he was right.

That evening, after a sumptuous dinner in the hotel's bar, Sam and Sid and Bill were relaxing in their suite, belching and sucking their teeth and drinking beer.

"Uurrp," said Sid or Sam.

"Uurrp," said Sam or Sid.

"Uurrp," said Bill.

This conversational brilliance went on for some time, until it was interrupted by a knock on the door. A gentle, delicate knock.

One of the S's was halfway to the door when Bill

remembered that he was expecting someone, even if he didn't know quite who. He dropped his beer, hauled himself off the sofa, and motored across the room, bowling Sid or Sam over in his rush.

Bill got the door open on the second try, once he remembered that he had to turn the knob. He swung the door wide, and there she stood.

Tall and slim, with flame-red hair down to her wasp-like waist, she stood there in the spangled evening gown she had been wearing at the auto show. If Bill's hands together could go around her waist, they would be challenged to encompass her breasts. Her legs rose up from the floor, and rose, and rose, until they made an ass of themselves. Bill couldn't see that, but he remembered it from this morning, and in form and motion it was, indeed, memorable.

He didn't remember her name as well as her bottom, but he wouldn't have been able to speak even if he did. She was a vision of incredible loveliness, compounded by the fact that Bill hadn't had any direct physical contact with a woman, aside from the nurse in the hospital, since at least the preceding volume in the series.

Fortunately, she took the initiative. "Kitty," she said. "We met this morning." She held out a perfect, sensuous hand languorously.

"Bill," he said. "With two L's."

"Of course." She looked into his eyes, and he felt something go soft deep inside. It was balanced by something else starting to go hard. "May I come in?"

"Bill," he said.

"I'll take that as yes."

Kitty moved Bill aside with a gentle touch of her hand and stepped into the room. "Are you busy with these gentlemen?" she asked.

"No, no, not at all. They were just leaving—right, guys?" Bill made subtle sweeping motions, waving both arms over his head to indicate to Sid and Sam that they should leave.

But this was not in their instructions.

"Gee. This isn't in our instructions," one of them said. "We were told to keep you out of trouble, and to keep you from doing anything that might offend your public."

Bill turned back to Kitty, pulled his tongue back into his mouth, and said, "You won't be offended, will you?" He shook his head vigorously back and forth.

"Not at all." She reached out with that perfect hand and stopped Bill's head which was still wagging. "I'm here of my own free will, and I'm over the age of consent."

Bill whispered what he could remember of a prayer of thanksgiving to Ahura-Mazda.

"Gee," one of the bodyguards said. "I guess it's OK then. Come on, Sid, we'll go into the other bedroom."

(*Got it!* Bill's subconscious said. *Sid is the one on the left! Sam is the one on the right!*)

Kitty undulated over to the sofa, sat down, and patted the cushion beside her. "Wouldn't you be more comfortable over here?"

"I'm not sure comfortable is exactly the right word," Bill said, running back across the room. It was particularly not comfortable because he forgot to go around the coffee table and had to limp the last few steps.

He sank down onto the couch and she swept him down and across his lap. "I love celebrities," she said.

Bill sighed. "I love being a celebrity."

The statuesque redhead put one hand on Bill's thigh and curled the other around his head. She gently lifted his head up and lowered her lips to his.

Kissing wasn't exactly what he'd had in mind when he put the room number on the pictures, but it was a good starting point, and Kitty was an especially good kisser. It was a promising beginning, and Bill could hardly wait to redeem the promise.

They had thrashed around into a full grapple when there was another knock on the door.

Kitty pulled away. "Are you expecting anyone? Room service, maybe?"

Bill pulled her back down. "No. Probably a wrong number."

Whoever it was knocked again, harder.

Bill tried to continue with the kissing, but Kitty's mouth was moving. "Are you sure that isn't for you?"

He shook his head. "No, not for me, no way, not a chance."

There was a third knock.

Sid or Sam—Bill still had no way of telling them apart if there was only one of them—stuck his head in from the bedroom. "Gee, Bill, should I get the door?"

"Uh—no, I'll get it." Resignedly, Bill disentangled his hand from the buttons on the back of Kitty's dress. Whoever it was, he'd just have to get rid of them quickly.

The door swung open to reveal a woman who was as beautiful as Kitty, but with short dark brown hair.

"Hello, Bill," she murmured. "Remember me? Misty?"

"Oh, yes," he sighed.

"You gave me an autographed picture this morning." She gave an unnecessary but delightful shimmy to remind him.

"Oh, yes," he sighed.

"May I come in?" Misty asked.

"Who's that, Bill?" Kitty asked.

"Oh, err, hmmm," Bill sighed.

"Is that you, Kitty?" Misty asked. She kissed Bill lightly on the cheek and stepped into the room. "Oh—am I interrupting anything?"

"Well, yes," Bill said. "I mean, actually, no." He tried to clear his head. He'd been raised to be polite, and he just couldn't figure out what was the polite thing to say in this situation. He also couldn't figure out how to keep both women here. He couldn't figure out how to explain to Kitty and Misty how they had both been invited. He couldn't figure out how Misty's simple little wraparound dress stayed attached to her body, except maybe magnetism or static electricity. He was altogether beyond rational thought or willful action.

"To tell you the truth, Misty," Kitty explained, "we were just about to get involved in strenuous heterosexuality."

Something deep inside Bill screamed in anguish. He'd been *pretty* sure that was what was going on, but you can never be absolutely certain of these things. Not in Bill's experience, anyway.

"Oh, goody!" Misty squealed. "Can I join you?" She touched a fastener somewhere and her dress fell apart and fluttered to the floor.

Bill was still paralyzed, but much happier now. He managed to get himself turned toward Kitty. "Please, please, uh-huh, uh-huh, please?"

But the redhead was already undoing the last of her buttons. Her dress didn't flutter to the floor; it was more of a slither. And unlike Misty, Kitty was wearing underwear, but it was all lace and frills, and in some ways even better than nothing.

Bill remembered a little more of that prayer.

In an instant he had a girl wrapped in each arm, nibbling at his exposed skin and working to expose more of it.

Kitty was pulling off his shirt, and Misty was working on the buckle of his trousers, when there was a tapping at the door.

Bill groaned.

The two women renewed and deepened their relationship while Bill put his shirt back on and answered the door.

"It's a bust!" A petite but voluptuous woman, with long straight black hair, opened her blouse. She was absolutely right.·

"It's *two* busts!" An Amazonian blonde jumped into the doorway and lifted her straining t-shirt.

Bill goggled, recovered, and led the two newcomers by their nipples into the room.

"Sue! Debbie!"

Bill looked from one pair of women to the other. "You all know each other?"

"Of course. Auto-show modeling is a small world," Misty explained. "Come on, girls, there's enough of this hunk to go around!"

Bill wasn't chancing any more interruptions. In a moment his clothes were scattered around the room, and he was so involved in nuzzling and nibbling and licking and groping and . . . well, and so on, that he didn't even hear the next knock on the door. Sam and Sid had to answer it.

There was only one woman there, but by the time Sid and Sam figured out what was going on and let her in, two more had shown up.

"Bill, could we talk to you for just a moment, please?"

"Can't it wait,"—he looked carefully and thought for a moment—"Sam?"

"No, it can't."

Sid picked up his left arm, Sam his right, and the bodyguards carried Bill women dripping off him, into the other bedroom.

"Gee, Bill, we're worried about you," Sid said.

"Absolutely," Sam said. "We have only your best interests at heart."

They set him down on the bed and crossed to a pair of chairs. Now the one that had been Sam became Sid, and vice versa.

"We understand that we can't intervene here," Sam said, "because of that Ginebra Convention you told us about."

"But we're worried about your health."

"Absolutely. It's your health that concerns us."

"We're afraid you might put too much of a strain on—"

"Your heart, that's it, your heart. All those women

may be too much for you."

"That's OK, guys," Bill said. "I'm used to taking risks. I'm a galactic hero, after all."

(NOTE: The following scene has been revised in accordance with an order from the Political Correctness Bureau. In the original version, Bill, Sam, and Sid revealed themselves to be self-centered, sexist pigs, and inappropriate role models. Bill offered his friends three of the women to use as sexual playthings, with no regard to the women's own desires and hopes for personal fulfillment as individuals.)

"But Bill," Sid said, "it will probably not be possible for you to completely satisfy seven women in one night."

"Correct," Sam said. "Particularly as we are sure you want to develop a deep and lasting personal relationship with each and every one of them."

"Yow!" said Bill. "You have prevented me from making a terrible mistake, in which I would be responsible for the base exploitation of my chance fame to degrade women for the satisfaction of my animal passions!" Bill wept manly tears.

## CHAPTER 12

WHEN HE THOUGHT ABOUT IT (WHICH wasn't for some time, considering that his brain power had been severely reduced by alcohol and they were still on the leg of the trip that included bars in the hotels), Bill did think it was funny that he hadn't been outside since he got into the ambulance back at the lake.

He also still hadn't figured out what the S-men had meant when they said "Uh-oh" to him some days earlier, because he hadn't seen much in the way of terrible destruction, or even anything to get seriously upset about.

But right now his main concern was, had he had a swinging time and plenty of booze the night before?

Because Bill had no memory of anything between when he walked into the room and when Sid and Sam shook him awake the next morning.

"Gee, Bill, it's time to get up. We've got another busy day ahead of us."

"Lemmallon," Bill mumbled into the pillow.

"No, Bill, we have to get going soon. One early stop

today, and then we start your USO tour of military bases and defense plants. Beauty queens, Bill. Chorus girls. The adulation of your fellow soldiers."

"Inawanna."

Sid lifted Bill's head from the pillow. "I can't believe I heard that correctly. Chorus girls, Bill."

Something small and atrophied stirred in the back of Bill's brain. It was his conscious mind, and it was gradually becoming aware that it didn't know what happened last night.

Under normal circumstances, this was no problem. The chief reason Bill had developed a taste for alcohol in the Troopers was so he could forget what he was doing, and had done, and was—namely, a Trooper. But normal circumstances had never before included the possible fulfillment of Bill's primary hormonal fantasy.

"Chorus girls," Bill croaked.

Sam slipped a straw between Bill's lips. Bill took a long pull, and screamed, "Eeyaughhhhhh!"

"Gee, Bill," Sam said apologetically, "I thought you liked boiling hot coffee in the morning."

"No' tha' ho'." But Bill was awake and upright now. He sucked cool air over his tongue and tried to speak again. "Last night . . . can't remember . . ."

Sid and Sam looked at each other. "You mean you don't recall a thing that happened?"

Bill shook his head morosely.

Sid looked at Sam and shrugged. "In that case, you had a wonderful time. You made love with many beautiful women in many interesting ways. Many times."

That had been Bill's dream, and he supposed he couldn't really complain if it had come true, but he made a small mental note that the next time it happened he wanted to be there. It wasn't quite as good, hearing about it secondhand.

Bill pumped his bodyguards and pals for all the details of the previous night's festivities while they hoisted him out of bed, into the sonic shower, and on through the whole morning routine that ended when they stuffed him into their hoverlimo. They earned their money, too, because not only was Bill utterly incapable of normal functioning this morning, so they even had to fork his food into his gaping mouth and brush his teeth for him, but they also had to make up the whole story.

They did such a wonderful job of inventing the story, in fact, that Bill had them tell it over and over again, in more and more detail. It kept getting better and better, until he could almost believe he remembered it himself. It was almost as good as if it had really happened.

It also kept Bill from noticing where they were going. Which was, among other things, outside.

He couldn't have seen much if he was looking, because the windows of the limo were tinted almost totally black, and what feeble bits of consciousness he possessed were far too devoted to learning about his exploits to care what they were passing.

Sam, on the other hand, had gotten totally bored with the story. He turned on the small holovideo set, hooked up an ear plug, and tuned in ENN. Bill paid no attention until he saw the little image of General Weissearse floating next to him.

"What's he got to say?"

"The same old crapola. The glorious forces of your glorious empire are fighting the glorious battle, gloriously. Bombing only military targets, no civilian casualties, no accidents, no imperial ships shot down. You want to hear it?"

Sam reached to switch the sound on, but Bill stopped him. "No, I've heard it before. In person, too. Wait— he means no *more* imperial ships shot down, right? Has he said anything about me?"

"No, of course not. If he admitted you exist, then he'd have to admit that we shot down your ship, and that would be admitting failure. So it didn't happen."

Bill brightened considerably at this news. "Does that mean I'm not a Trooper any more? I mean, if I don't exist, I can't be a Trooper. Is that like a discharge?" Since no one was ever discharged from the Troopers, Bill was unfamiliar with the procedure.

"Gee, Bill, I doubt it."

"And why do you guys keep saying 'gee'? I used to know someone else who said that all the time, and he was a Chinger spy."

Sid laughed. "Gee, Bill, since I'm not a seven-foot-tall green lizard, I don't think I could be a Chinger. Anyway, we must have picked it up from President Grotsky. He uses it a lot, and we spend most of the time guarding him."

"I guess that could be it," Bill muttered, only half convinced. "What's that?"

The floating image of General Weissearse had been replaced by a picture of an Eyerackian airfield, shot from very high up. The camera was zooming toward the airfield at an incredible speed.

Sam pulled out the ear plug jack and the sound came back on.

"This bit of film was selected entirely at random, and has not been edited or altered in any way," the General was saying. "As you can see, the camera is in the nose of one of our newest types of missiles, the Peacemaker Mark XXXVII. It has a computer that has been programmed to emulate the mind of a highly trained Trooper, with all the latest artificial stupidity techniques.

"Now, you see that red dot that just appeared in the middle of your picture? That marks the firing mechanism for an ASS battery. If we just blow up the firing mechanism, the missiles don't blow up and hardly anyone is killed; only the man at the trigger, if he doesn't get clear in time."

The picture looked pretty familiar to Bill. Except for all the strangely flat spaces around the airfield, which looked like they had been drawn in with a crayon, it was just like the view from his turret on the *Heavenly*

*Peace*. Bill waited for the little "50," the score for an ASS battery, to come up, but it didn't.

"You can see how the red dot stays right in the middle of the picture," General Weissearse continued. "There is no deviation from plan, no possibility of error.

"If you'll look closely at the end here, and we'll slow down the tape to make it easier, you can see that the ASS ground crew can see and hear the Peacemaker Mark XXXVII coming, and they have plenty of time to get clear of the blast."

The picture did slow down, and the missile curved in and aimed for a door. A crudely hand-lettered sign on the door read "Eyerackian Space Defense Command: Legitimate Military Target." There was a red and white bull's-eye below the sign.

Then the door flew open, and three men dashed out, loping like moon-walkers in the slow motion. There was an extreme close-up of the sign, and the tape was finished.

"As you can see, this randomly selected piece of tape, which is absolutely typical of the millions of missiles that we are launching against the atheistic warmongering Eyerackian military establishment, clearly demonstrates the precision of our attack, and the care we are taking not to harm any of the innocent and oppressed citizens of Eyerack, who are the emperor's beloved subjects.

"This should put to rest any doubts and rumors to the effect that there are any Eyerackian civilian casualties, other than a few people who have been disturbed by the noise."

The tiny image of the General floated smugly inside the hoverlimo until Sam shut off the holovideo.

"You believe him?" he asked Bill.

"He's an officer," Bill replied.

Sam looked puzzled. "I don't follow."

"We don't have much experience with officers," Sid explained.

"A rule of the Troopers is that anything an officer says is probably a lie at best; at worst he is out to kill you."

"Ah," said Sid and Sam.

"You guys have a lot to learn about being at war."

"We're picking it up pretty fast," Sam claimed.

"Not so much that we're picking it up," Sid clarified, "as that it's falling on us."

The hoverlimo slowed down and pulled over.

"We're here. No autographs at this one, Bill."

"No autographs?"

"No, Bill."

"No models?"

"No, Bill."

"No chorus girls?"

"Not at this stop. Here you just have to lay a wreath." Bill grinned. "No, that's *not* what I mean! A wreath, a big bunch of flowers. The local mayor will hand it to you when you get out. You take it and march up to the monument. You stop in front of the monument for a moment, as though you're feeling sad, and you say, 'In honor of the dead.' Then you place the wreath carefully at the base of the monument and walk slowly back here. Got it?"

Bill concentrated for a minute. "Sure. 'In honor of the dead.' No problem. I know a lot of people who are dead."

There was a big crowd waiting, but not like the other crowds Bill had seen. This one was quiet, and it stayed behind the barricades without pushing forward or reaching out to touch Bill. A roundish man in a black suit came up, shook Bill's hand, and introduced himself as the mayor of the city. Bill didn't know what city it was, and the name wouldn't have meant anything to him in any case, so he just nodded politely and took the wreath.

Attached to the wreath was a big ribbon, and someone had thoughtfully inscribed Bill's line on it. He started to tuck it under one arm, but Sam whispered from behind him that he should hold it out at arm's length so everyone could see it. That was a little awkward, but the wreath wasn't too heavy.

The hard part was walking down that long, wide aisle through the silent crowd. Every one of the thousands of faces was turned toward Bill, watching and waiting. It was a lot harder on his nerves than the screaming throngs he'd seen before. Those were a little like combat, and he knew how to deal with it. This was more like the time before a battle, when you didn't really know what to expect, except that it wouldn't be good.

The monument wasn't right at the end of the aisle, but off to the left a little. Right at the end was a big pile of rubble. Bill couldn't look around much—every time he tried to turn his head Sid or Sam would whisper "Eyes front!" and, trained to obey or get clobbered as he was, he would look straight ahead. But what he could see of the area seemed to include a lot of other big piles of rubble, and buildings whose tops had been blown off, and, on one side of the aisle, one big crater that had partly filled with water. It looked like someone had bombed the bowb out of this town.

Bill finally got to the end of the long avenue between the barricades. The big pile of rubble had once been a building, and not too long ago, to judge by the rescue crews standing beside it, still sweaty and grimy. A big metal sign, twisted and with a hole in the middle, lay on the ground nearby. Despite its condition, Bill could read it easily.

AIR-RAID SHELTER—MAXIMUM CAPACITY 600 CIVILIANS was what it said.

Bill executed a smart left-face and took the few steps up to the monument as slowly as he could. He knew where he'd seen that sign before; could it be a coincidence that he was seeing it again?

The monument was just some more rubble, but welded together into a small column. Engraved into the plasteel girders was a long list of names.

*INTERMISSION*

Ahh, the wonders of Technology! We become so used to our electronic gadgets that we hardly notice when our TV set begins to wash the dishes—or when our telephone whispers lewd remarks. Commonplace!

What is not commonplace is the continual advance of camera technology. Would you believe that a camera as small as a grain of rice can make a picture of the Statue of Liberty that is just as big as the Statue of Liberty? You believe *that*? There's one like you born every minute.

Yet there really are tiny, strong, incredibly exotic, unbelievable cameras such as the ones that follow...

## FOOTLOCKER

Photographed by a secret flying camera disguised as a mosquito (so realistic you can get malaria if stung by the camera). Bill now has an incredible collection of fake feet—one for every occasion.

## ANTIGRAV SUIT

An exciting combat photograph (taken by a flying camera disguised as a pigeon; so realistic it makes pigeon doo-doo). Those explosions are real explosions and Bill's expression of petrified terror is equally real.

SID, SAM, ETC.

A rather unusual photograph of Sid, Sam, and friends. They are scowling because the camera that took this photo was disguised as a louse on the back of a hairy head. They have seen it and are all afraid of getting crabs.

BILL BENT VIA CROSSBOW

Bill's adventures border on the ludicrous at times. If this picture had not been photographed from the frontal lobes of a mental telepath it could have been considered rather impossible.

STRAFING FIRE

An interesting photo taken by a camera disguised as an armor piercing shell. A microsecond before it exploded, it ejected this photo.

BILL'S COED GIRL

In the name of good taste, something usually lacking in this narrative, a cloak of secrecy will be drawn over the circumstances involving this photo.

SKATEBOARD BILL

You will notice—and appreciate—the grace with which
Bill has mastered his skateboarding technique. The
camera that took this, disguised as a roach, was
unhappily mashed an instant later; the undamaged
negative was salvaged from the crushed husk.

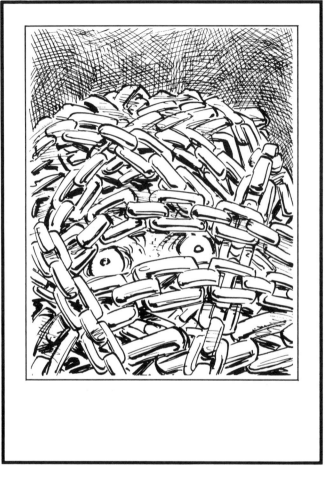

BILL IN CHAINS

It goes without saying, but we will say it anyway, that
the camera that took this picture was disguised as a link
of chain.

BGR MAKES HIS APPEARANCE

This photo of Bgr was taken by a Chinger photographer, which is why he looks so good instead of like a loathsome alien. Happily the photographer was wasted an instant later and the camera retrieved and washed clean.

## SPEECH-MAKING BILL

In a galaxy filled with boring speech-makers, Bill is seen here fighting for bottom place. Photo taken by accident when the photographer fell asleep and his chin touched the button.

BILL WITH CELEBRATING GIRLS

This disgustingly heterosexual photograph was taken by a camera disguised as an olive in a martini, which was eaten a moment later and eventually retrieved in a manner we're unable to disclose in this family publication.

OLD PROSPECTOR

The camera that took this picture was disguised as a camera—which did not fool the mule, who smiled for his picture.

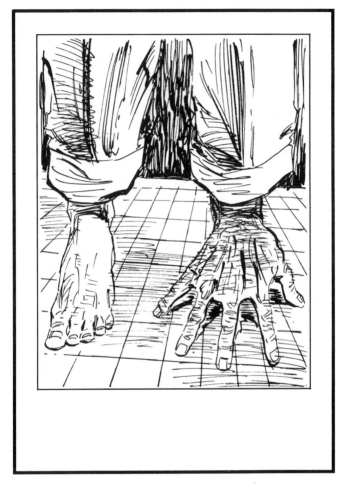

## FOOT AND HAND

The end of a wild foot is always a tragedy. But at least
the new foot is handy...

Bill leaned the wreath gently up against the base of the column and said, "In honor of the dead," just as he'd been instructed. He stood at attention and gave his unique two-handed salute.

All the way to their next stop on the tour, Sam and Sid couldn't get him to say anything.

## CHAPTER 13

BILL ZIGZAGGED ACROSS THE PARKING LOT, hurdling a couple of small craters, his instincts telling him when to swerve away from an incoming bomb and when to dive into a larger crater for cover. One more large explosion, and he leaped out and forward again. He looked back and waved an arm to summon his comrades. "Follow me," he shouted.

He vaulted an overturned hovercar and ducked behind it to see if they were coming.

Sam and Sid weren't nearly as good at this as Bill was, but they were getting the hang of it. Fortunately, the Imperial Troopers weren't strafing; they weren't even attacking seriously. The bodyguards caught up, but before they could catch their breath Bill led them on a final dash across the last few yards into one of the few buildings still standing.

The two Eyerackians collapsed, gasping, into the nearest chairs. Bill, however, had not yet reached his goal, and he marched up to the counter.

"Three SuperHestburgers, three double beers. Fast,"

he said. "To stay." He turned back to Sid and Sam. "What do you guys want?"

An explosion rattled the windows, and the girl behind the counter ducked for cover. By the time she re-emerged, Bill had the rest of his order. "One Chilly-Chili, One Horse Dog, a large Tranqui-Cola."

He carried the trays over to their table.

"Gee, Bill, we were sure lucky."

"Yeah, imagine finding an open Burger Barn. I haven't had a burger since . . . since . . . maybe I've never had one before. But I've seen the commercials!" Bill washed down the first burger with the first beer, in one gulp each.

The girl behind the counter turned on the holovision. A miniature President Grotsky, a little thinner than when Bill had met him and looking more than ever just like Sam and Sid, stood on the counter. "The war is going about as well as can be expected," he said, "under the circumstances. Casualties are pretty high on both sides, and there's a lot of nasty stuff falling out of the sky all over—rockets, bombs, shrapnel, pieces of airplanes and spaceships. I really suggest you stay indoors. The underground malls and tunnel trains are a good idea. Personally, I'm planning on staying in my bunker for the time being."

"Gee, poor old Millard doesn't sound terribly inspirational, does he, Sid?"

"No, Sam, he doesn't. But he is under a lot of pressure, after all."

"True enough, Sid. But at least he doesn't have to eat at Burger Barn." Sam poked reluctantly at his Horse Dog. "I don't think there's even any real horse in this thing."

"Doesn't *have* to?" Bill said with artificial ingredients dripping down his chin. "All this stuff is made from real processed meat-like food-type product. You can't get anything this good in the Troopers."

Sid nodded. "That explains why they're so aggressive."

Bill shoveled the last of his meal into his mouth, chewed two or three times, and swallowed. "Uuurrrppp," he eructed. "That was good. What's our next stop?"

"The neutron mine. At least we'll be safe there. Everything's underground, including the barracks where we'll be staying. Some of the bombs were a little too close for comfort last night."

"You worry too much. They didn't even come close to the hotel." After a week of touring in areas that were under attack, Bill had gotten blasé about it. Since nobody was really aiming at him, he didn't take it as personally as he did when he was still aboard the *Heavenly Peace*. Although secretly he was happily looking forward to getting into a nice, safe, deep mine.

Sam gathered the trays and carried them over to the recycling bin, where the trash would be reprocessed into more Grundgeburgers. He stopped at the counter to see General Weissearse's latest press briefing on the holovision.

A junior officer introduced him. "Heeeere's Wormy!"

A military band played the general's theme music, the reporters broke into applause, and Stormy Wormy Weissearse came through the curtains onto the stage. He let the applause go on for a while, then said "Thank you, thank you." As the crowd grew quiet, he continued, "How many Eyerackians does it take to screw in a light bulb?"

The press corps, right on cue, shouted in unison, "How many?"

"Only two, but they have to be really tiny."

The mandatory uproarious laughter stopped at the general's signal.

"In the last twenty-four hours, Imperial forces launched just over twelve million missions against Eyerack, bringing the total for the war so far to nearly one hundred fifty million. Almost the entire Eyerackian air defense was eliminated five days ago, but six missiles were fired at Imperial ships from mobile launchers today.

"Our precision bombing was concentrated on defense industries today. We have a randomly selected and completely unedited tape to show the results of one of these attacks."

General Weissearse was replaced on the counter top by the same picture Bill and the bodyguards had seen earlier. The missile, this time described as a smart bomb guided by remote control, bored in on the same red dot. The sign on the building was different, though. Now it read "MISSILE FACTORY: LEGITIMATE MILITARY TARGET."

"We have an unconfirmed report of a teenaged girl being bruised by a piece of falling litter that was accidentally ejected from one of our bombers. If this turns out to be correct, that will bring the total of Eyerackian civilian casualties to two since the beginning of the campaign. Anything else you may have heard is only enemy propaganda.

"A turret gunner on the Imperial Cruiser *Bomfog* sustained a blister on his trigger finger. This makes seven injuries of all sorts to Imperial forces. No ships have been shot down. Anything else you may have heard is only enemy propaganda.

"The campaign is going exactly according to plan. Anything else you may have heard is only enemy propaganda."

Sam joined Sid and Bill by the door.

Bill pointed up into the sky. "We're just waiting for that dog fight to finish." A light rain of spent bullets and debris was pocking what was left of the pavement outside. There was a small explosion far above. "Fighter," Bill murmured. "Yours." Moments later, another small explosion. "Yours again." Tiny dots maneuvered around in the blue, only slightly obscured by smoke. Bill's practiced eye, and a fair assurance that the other two wouldn't know enough to contradict anything he said, let him describe the action. The sound effects might not have been strictly necessary, but they were fun to make. "*Ack-ack-ack! Kabloom! Ka-bloom! Phloosh! Spang! Spang!*"

At last there was another explosion, larger than the others. "Escort destroyer," Bill said. "Imperial. That does it. Let's go."

They sprinted a couple of hundred yards across the cratered parking lot to the armored hoverlimo, which hadn't been able to get any closer to the Burger Barn. The car hadn't taken much damage while they were eating—only a couple of new dents in the roof; that right headlight had been broken a couple of days earlier.

The rest of the trip to the neutron mine was basically uneventful. They were strafed twice, blown off the road once by a nearby bomb, had to ford two rivers where bridges had ceased to exist, and six times had to cross fields and frontyards for stretches of up to five Imperial miles because the road had been churned to the consistency of cottage cheese. All in all, they made the trip of fifty miles in less than four hours.

Most mines have a lot of equipment by the entrance, to handle the ore or whatever they are bringing to the surface, but not this one. Neutrons, after all, are very small, and lots and lots of them can go in a fairly small package. So a neutron mine (or at least this one, and this one was, after all, the only one in the universe), from the outside, looked like a road leading into an underground parking garage. An underground parking garage with armed sentries and blastproof armored doors.

The blast doors swung open into a clean, well-lighted chamber. The only other mine Bill had ever seen was a guano mine he'd toured as part of his preliminary training to be a Technical Fertilizer Operator (his greatest non-hormonal dream, now, alas, never to be fulfilled), and this one looked nothing like that one. For one thing, the place was not covered with guano dust. Despite his deep appreciation for fertilizer in all its forms, Bill really had to consider this an advantage.

The neutron mine, in fact, looked more like a factory—at least in its upper levels. There actually was a parking garage, and after that a small room with a receptionist in a skin-tight jumpsuit. She was studiously ignoring the visitors, but Bill had difficulty ignoring her. She was a little on the plumpish side, but definitely pneumatic, with masses of curly blonde hair. She was everything Bill looked for in a woman; which is to say, she was a woman.

Bill sidled up to the reception desk to meet the receptionist, but Sid cut him off at the pass. Or actually, before he could make a pass.

"Sid and Sam, Presidential Guards, with Bill, Celebrity Prisoner of War, to see the director. He's expecting us."

The receptionist put her romance holonovel on pause, took off her earphones, popped her gum, and looked the trio over. "Not in those outfits. We run a respectable neutron mine here." She slapped a bell on her desk and called, "Front!" A small robot popped out of the wall and rolled over. "You'll find cleansuits in the closet. Everyone wears cleansuits in here. Keep them sealed at all times. Don't try to smuggle any neutrons out of the mine. Got it?" Without waiting for a response, she told the robot, "Take these three to guest suite 8, make sure they change, and bring them back here. Dismissed." She popped her gum again and picked up the earphones.

"What about our luggage?" Sam asked.

The receptionist sighed, put down her earphones again, and looked at the men. "I don't see any luggage."

"It's in the car."

"You can worry about that after you see the director. He's expecting you in ten minutes, and you've just wasted thirty seconds of it." She jammed the earphones on her head and started the holonovel again. Tiny half-clothed translucent figures grappled on top of her desk.

The robot was already halfway down the hall, going around a corner. They caught it just before it got on the elevator, then followed it through a maze of hallways and into a small suite.

It was called a suite, but it didn't have much in common with a hotel besides having two bedrooms and a living room. The entire space, including the furniture, had apparently been extruded in one piece. It was soft and cozy, as far as plasticrete went, which wasn't very far. It was sturdy and durable—you could take a sledgehammer to any of the chairs without doing any damage—and about as comfortable as a rock.

"You have two minutes and eighteen seconds to change your clothes," the robot intoned. "Then I will lead you back to the reception desk. Brevet Lance Corporal Bill, your room is on the right." It retracted its legs and displayed a countdown clock showing how much time they had left.

Bill rushed into his room, ripping off his clothes as he went. Selecting a new outfit was easy—he could take one of the white cleansuits, or another one. They were all the same. He did appreciate the chevron that had been painted on the sleeve, though.

Just over two minutes later, Bill and his bodyguards were hopping down the hallway after the robot, still pulling on their suits and trying to figure out how to seal the seams. When they got to the front desk again, they were holding the cleansuits together with two hands.

The receptionist looked up at them, popped her eyes and took in their predicament. "Look," she said, standing, "it's simple." She demonstrated on herself; Bill paid especially close attention, although not to the process she was teaching. "Just press here and here, slide your hand along here, rub these two together, press here, and pull here. Got it?" Sam and Sid looked blank. Bill looked excited. But somehow they got themselves sealed up.

A bell chimed on the desk, and a door slid open in the corner. The receptionist sat down again. "The director will see you now." She turned all her attention back to her holonovel.

The door slid shut behind them, sealing the trio into a small room of the same style as their suite. It was the same extruded plasticrete, with one bench. They perched tentatively on the bench, facing the only variation in the room, a large square smooth patch on the wall.

"THANK YOU, THANK YOU, THANK YOU!" A disembodied voice blasted out of nowhere. "Sorry, Let me turn down the volume. It's a real honor to have you here, let me tell you."

Bill looked around. "Am I missing something?" he asked in a whisper.

"I don't think so," Sid replied.

"Nope. Nothing," Sam said.

"Can't you see me?" the voice said, "Right here. Gee, I forgot to turn on the video, didn't I?" The big smooth patch flickered and turned into a picture of a man sitting at a desk. "That's better, isn't it?" He was bald, with just a fringe of hair, and obviously well-fed, but otherwise he was another member of the look-alike set that included President Millard Grotsky, Sam, Sid, and all the other bodyguards. They all had the same mustache, the same dark hair. Bill wondered if a cloning machine had gone berserk somewhere on Eyerack thirty or forty years ago.

And he said "gee," too. Bill didn't even bother to ask about it this time.

"Gee, Bill, you haven't changed," the director said.

"Have I met you before?" Bill asked.

"Oh, no, I mean from your pictures on the news. I'm Snorri Yakamoto. I'm really happy to meet you."

Bill looked around at the cell-like room. What he could see of the director's office in the wall screen looked like genuine woodoid furniture, plastic-grain paneling on the walls, and a window. "I guess so. Nice office."

"Thanks. Gee, I won't be able to meet you personally, but I've told Sylvia to do everything to make you feel at home, and to make sure you get the real VIP treatment while you're here."

"Sylvia?"

"My receptionist. She's really something, isn't she?"

Bill felt he could agree with that.

"We'll have a dinner for you, and then tomorrow you'll get a tour of the whole mine. How does that sound?"

"Thrilling," Bill said unthrillingly.

The dinner lived up to Bill's expectations.

The extruded dining room looked like any number of mess halls where Bill had eaten before. Robots served the meals instead of diners having to line up at a service counter, but they still came on trays, and all the supposedly different parts were gray and indistinguishable and mixed together at the edges.

The other guests were all tired and monosyllabic after their day's work. Bill did get to sit next to Sylvia, the only woman in the room, but every time his hand even started to move toward her knee, she punched him in the side of the head. And that was the only attention she paid to him, being still absorbed in her holoromance.

In short, the high point of the evening for Bill was when they went back to the car for their luggage.

"Gee, Bill," Sam said, "at least you know tomorrow will be restful."

# CHAPTER 14

"*BLAAAT! BLAAAT! BLAAAT!*"

The alarm trilled gently in Bill's ear.

"*Burrrp! Blunnk! Bzzzzz!*"

He sat bolt upright and grabbed for the controls of his turret before he remembered where he was. Then he reminded himself that, no matter what else could be said against the neutron mine, no one was trying to kill him here. He sighed, stretched, and leaned back against the extruded plasticrete pillow.

"*Blaaat! Blaaat! Blaaat!*"

Bill reached out and dealt a mighty blow to the alarm. The plasticrete alarm ignored the blow. Rubbing his hand, Bill had no choice remaining other than to get up.

The alarm shut off automatically.

Bill stumbled out into the living room of the suite and sat heavily on the couch. "Ow!" He shifted position to rub his butt.

Sid or Sam came out of his room, already through with the sonic shower and struggling with his cleansuit.

"Gee, Bill, you'd better get a move on. That robot'll be here pretty soon, and it won't wait for you to get dressed."

"Rrrmmph."

Sam or Sid grabbed Bill's right arm—that is, the right arm on the right side—and pulled him upright. "Am I going to have to put you in the shower again?"

"Rrrmmph. No." Bill dragged himself back to his bedroom, and got back out, cleansuit hanging off him, with nearly a minute to spare. Sid (they were both out now, so Bill could tell them apart) sealed him up.

"Today you will tour the mine," the robot said by way of greeting. "Follow me." It rotated and left.

Sylvia met them under a big sign that said ADIT.

"Adit?" Bill asked.

"Snorri's a big crossword puzzle fan."

"Oh," Bill said, no less confused.

"This neutron mine is unique in the universe," Sylvia began her prepared speech. "Although all sorts of weapons can be built without neutrons, they are absolutely essential to the production of neutron bombs. Therefore neutron mining is controlled by the government as a strategic industry. Unauthorized removal of neutrons from this mine is a felony, punishable by a life sentence of hard labor in the lowest levels of the mine. Each of you will be given a souvenir neutron at the conclusion of this tour, but taking even one additional one will be treated as a crime."

The adit doors slid open, and they went down a ramp into the mine proper. It looked very much like the hallways of a very cheap hotel. Except for being sprayed on rather than extruded, it was just like the upper levels.

"No expense has been spared to make working conditions as pleasant as possible, as you can see. As the neutron deposits are depleted, the upper levels are turned into residential, office, and laboratory space."

Sylvia opened a door and let the visitors look in. Bill maneuvered around until he was directly behind her, and without looking she punched him in the right arm. "In here, scientists are working on improved ways of tracing the neutron veins through the surrounding rock." A few sad-looking people with white lab coats over their cleansuits sat around a table. Sylvia closed the door before they even registered her presence.

"These elevators take miners down to the actual working levels. There are three types of levels: exploration, in the very deepest and newest parts of the mine; production, in those areas where exploration has been completed; and reclamation, where the veins have been mined out and the levels are being prepared for other uses. We will be going to the main production level, two miles below the surface."

They all stood silently in the elevator as it descended. Bill yawned. Sam picked it up, then Sid, and Sylvia passed it back to Bill. This went on for a while, until Bill said, "You know, I'm a celebrity. People are nice to me wherever I go." Sylvia punched him in the arm. "That's not what I mean. How come the director can't greet us personally?"

"The director doesn't see anyone personally," Sylvia said.

"Not even President Grotsky," Sid said thoughtfully. "And they're good friends. The president appointed Yakamoto to this job, and he's never seen him except on the holophone."

"That's weird," Bill commented.

"Snorri says he's worried about diseases," Sylvia explained.

"I'm clean!" Bill objected.

Sylvia looked at him and snorted.

"No, really! I shower all the time. Sid and Sam can vouch for me."

Sylvia raised an eyebrow. "Really? So that's how it is."

This would have continued indefinitely, but the elevator reached their level.

As they stepped out, Sylvia slipped back into her tour-guide mode. Bill wasn't sure if that was an improvement.

"Since neutrons are so small, in their natural state they tend to be mixed up with lots of other small things, like sand, dust, and pebbles. A great deal of the space on the production levels, therefore, must be devoted to the equipment that separates the neutrons from the scree."

"Scree?" Bill asked.

"Snorri likes crossword puzzles.

"Behind this soundproofed wall on your left is the sorting room. This is the largest single room in the mine. Please stay close to me." She punched Bill on the arm. "Not that close."

The din when she opened the door was impressive. The conveyor belts and cranes and trucks moving around were loud enough, but the vast sorter drowned them out.

The sorter was one huge machine stretching almost the whole length of the room, nearly half a mile. At various points different grades of ore were being dumped and shoveled and scooped into it, from fairly large boulders at the beginning to sand near the end. Sylvia couldn't explain anything above the noise, but it was clear enough that she just had to point to the main features through the clouds of rock and neutron dust, and even Bill could understand it.

Each section worked pretty much the same. The ore was thrown down a hopper, which fed it onto a large, heavy screen. The screen was shaken until everything that could fall through had done so. What remained on top was fed off to be crushed and sent through the hopper again with the next load. What fell through went into the next hopper, which went onto the next smallest screen. It was all incredibly noisy and even more boring; Bill felt his eyelids closing.

The shaking, shoveling, and crushing went on until the powder was so fine it was almost like a liquid, and only the neutrons themselves could get through the last screen. They fell into the industrial shipping containers like a mist. Workmen periodically stopped the rain of neutrons, sealed the containers, and put empty boxes in place. Guards watched the containers. Technicians with neutron detectors and really big magnifying glasses watched everyone else, making sure no stray neutrons rolled away, got caught in the seams of the cleansuits, or got stolen.

"Next," Sylvia announced when they were back in the hallway again, "we will see how the neutron ore is extracted."

But before they could get to that, a voice came over the public address system. "Brevet Lance Corporal Bill, please pick up any white courtesy phone. Brevet Lance Corporal Bill, any white courtesy phone, please."

"Me?" Bill asked. "Who knows I'm here?"

"Gee, Bill, it has been in all the newspapers," Sam whined.

"Oh, yeah. You told me. All I read is the funnies."

Sylvia led Bill to the nearest phone and stood a discreet distance away.

"Hello, Bill here."

"Gee, Bill, where are you?"

"President Grotsky? Is that you? I'm in the mine."

"No, Bill, this is Snorri, the director, remember? What part of the mine are you in?"

Bill looked around and tried to remember what he'd just seen. "I'm outside a big room with a lot of machinery."

"The sorting room. Main production level. Well then, you have about five minutes before the soldiers come to arrest you. You can't get out, but you may be able to hide somewhere down there. Take Sam and Sid with you, OK?"

"Hide? Why? I'm a celebrity; I don't hide from people."

"Gee, Bill, you aren't a celebrity any more. Now

you're an enemy soldier. There's been a military coup, and the new government wants to make you a prisoner. Well, they're trying to break down my door now. Gotta go!" And soon-to-be-former-director Yakamoto hung up.

"Sylvia! Where's the back entrance?"

Sylvia popped her gum. "Nowhere. There's only one entrance, you know. Why?"

"There's been a takeover by the military. They're coming here after me and Sid and Sam. You too, I bet. We've gotta hide!"

Sylvia popped her gum again. "What do you mean 'we,' paleface? I just work here. What about Snorri?"

"They were breaking down his door when he hung up."

"Well, until they get here I still work for him. I gotta warn you, though, when the new guys show up I work for them. Your best bet is the exploration levels. Those aren't mapped so well."

Bill grabbed the bodyguards and explained on the way to the elevator.

The bottom level of the mine wasn't nearly as luxurious as the production level. The walls hadn't been sprayed with plasticrete yet, the air conditioning hadn't been installed, there were very few lights, and the place generally looked like a mine.

"This way," Bill said, picking a direction at random.

Within moments they were lost in the darkness.

# CHAPTER 15

"SAM?"

No answer.

"Sid?"

Still no answer.

"Bill?" Bill said.

"Yeah?"

Well, Bill thought, at least *I'm* here.

He had no idea where *here* was, or how long he'd been here, or how to get out, but at least he knew something.

He also knew that the soldiers hadn't found him, and that had to count for something, too. But not much, since the soldiers would have been able to give him food, and he hadn't found any of that down here. He'd fallen into lots of puddles, so water wasn't a problem, but he was getting really hungry; he was just about hungry enough to start considering giving himself up.

In fact, he'd already started thinking about considering it. He could tell that his beard was coming in, and that meant he had been wandering around in the dark for three or four days, at least. And his last meal was the evening before that. The food hadn't been very good, but it was getting better and better in retrospect. Bill was almost at the point where Trooper food would start looking good.

He stumbled slowly along, hands in front of him to keep from smashing his nose against the walls too often. Crunch! There was another one. He looked in both directions, just as a matter of form. It had been a long time since he'd seen anything; the place was, appropriately, as dark as the bottom of a mine.

To the right? Just what he expected—nothing. To the left? He must be going blind. A pale spot floated in front of him. He rubbed his eyes. The spot was still there. But wait! He remembered that he'd seen something like that before. It was a thing called a light!

Without thinking about it—as though that was something different in Bill's life—he staggered toward the distant glow.

He stumbled slowly at first, but gradually the implications of his discovery penetrated his granitic mind and moved him faster. If he didn't follow this light and get some food soon, he would die. And if he was dead, running away from the soldiers would not have done him any good. In that case, he might as well be a prisoner.

At the worst, being a prisoner couldn't be much worse than being a trooper, could it? And it had to be at least a little bit better than slowly dying of starvation in the darkness.

Staggering, stumbling and falling, always moving forward, toward the speck of light, Bill started to pick up speed. Eventually the light got bright enough so that he could make out the side walls of the passage; he accelerated to a medium shamble.

Now he could see the floor, at least enough to pick out the larger rocks and pits. He pressed on, pouring all his strength into reaching that light before it vanished;

before it left him alone to die in the dark. Desperation drove him to almost a normal walking pace.

The speck of light grew, becoming a small yellow ball, drawing him ever on, bringing on pungent hallucinations of food smells: coffee, beer, beans, and bacon. As he neared it, he became certain he was having some kind of psychotic episode, that's what the shrinks called it. Brought on, no doubt, by stress, hunger, and disorientation. Either that or he'd gone completely around the bend.

Yes, that had to be it. What other explanation could there be for a campfire in a mine? Perhaps the short, grizzled old man squatting by the fire could tell Bill. Or if not him, maybe his burro knew a thing or two.

As he got near, Bill was impressed with the consistency of the hallucination. The fire gave off heat, the bacon popped in the pan, and the old man smelled as though he couldn't even spell the word bath.

Just because the man was a hallucination, though, was no reason not to be polite. "Excuse me, Mr. Hallucination," Bill began, "my name is Bill."

"Eh?" The old man looked up from under the broad brim of his hat, hooked a thumb in the strap of his overalls, and asked, "What can I do for you, sonny?"

"I know you're just a figment of my starved imagination, sir, but could you possibly spare some of that make-believe food? I'd be very grateful."

"I ain't no hallucination, sonny. I'm a prospector. Can't you tell? Burro, beard, overalls, bacon and beans, campfire? Heh heh heh," he heh-hehed. "Those are the sure signs of the stereotypical prospector right down through history, and that's what I am, dagnabbit. Gabby Gormless, prospector. Got a union card here somewheres." The hallucination searched through his pockets in vain. "But hunker on down by the fire. Here's a plate and spoon."

Bill had never hunkered before, and in his weakened state it wasn't an easy skill to master, but he didn't worry about it. After all, if he pitched face-first into the fire, he'd only hit his head on bare rock, since it was a hallucination. And he'd taken enough blows to the head in the past that it would be a familiar experience.

Still, the tin plate seemed real enough, and the beans, right out of the cookpot, felt as though they were burning his mouth. In a lifetime that had seen its share of hallucinatory experiences, this one was remarkably realistic. But among the many useful skills Bill had picked up in the Troopers was the ability to ignore completely the difference between fantasy and reality, which in the Troopers didn't really exist, so he just enjoyed it and tried not to think about all the sinister implications.

The chief implication, of course, was that he was dying. Considering how much work he'd put into not dying, if Bill had let himself think about this he would have found it terribly unfair. Not to mention depressing. So he didn't think about it.

He just settled in and enjoyed his hallucination. It was wonderful how the illusory beans seemed to taste so good, and the bacon seemed to be just on the borderline between tender and crisp, and the coffee—the coffee seemed to be real coffee, without acorns or petroleum byproducts or any kind of recycled fillers. And the beer for afters, really beery beer. That was the part that convinced Bill it had to be a hallucination. Even though the apparent second portion seemed to fill him up, and he seemed to have more energy after he finished, he knew that all this was an illusion.

So was the great belch that followed.

"You must 'o been right hungry, there, young feller."

Bill sucked his teeth and considered. He had just eaten an entirely imaginary meal, and now his equally imaginary host wanted to strike up a conversation. Definitely—the signs pointed toward completely woo-woo.

But when insane, as the saying goes . . .

"Yep, pretty hungry. You're a hallucination of mine, aren't you?"

"Waall, sonny, it don't feel that way to me, but I suppose it wouldn't, if'n I were your hallucination. Interesting epistemological question, ain't it? Like the one about am I a man awaking from a dream of being a butterfly, or a butterfly dreaming I'm a man."

"I don't know that one," Bill said. "How does it go?"

"Never mind. Old Zen parable. But what about you? What brings you down here? How long you been wandering around without food or lights?"

"Gee, I don't know."

The illusory prospector gave Bill a piercing look. "Consarn it, I useta know a feller who said 'gee' all the time. 'Course, he was a lot shorter than you. But that's another matter. How come you don't know how long you been here? Seems the kind o' thing a feller should know."

Bill felt a little silly, humoring someone who didn't exist, but he had nothing better to do. "I've been down here since the coup. I ran away from the soldiers with my two friends Sam and Sid so we wouldn't get arrested, and I lost them—that is, the soldiers, but then also Sid and Sam. Ever since then, I've been looking for them and trying to stay away from the search parties."

"Have you seen any search parties?"

"No, not really, but I've heard some people in the distance who might have been looking for me."

"I see. So why'd you come up to my campfire?"

"You're not real," Bill explained.

"Waall, I reckon that makes sense." The imaginary geezer chuckled. "So tell me about this dang coup. When'd it happen, and who got overthrown? I been out here in the tunnels for a month, completely out o' touch. Is Snorri Yakamoto out of a job?"

"Last I heard, they were breaking down his door. But the coup was against President Grotsky."

"The generals got Millard!" Gabby seemed genuinely shocked. "It musta been the generals. 'N if'n they wuz after you, you must be a pal o' Millard's, right?"

"Sort of. We had a few beers together."

"Waall, that's good enough fer me! I'm gonna do what I can to help you! Just tell me what you want."

What the hey, Bill thought. There was no harm in talking to the guy. What could the guy do to Bill, if he wasn't real? Maybe get him out of this mine. Sure, why not ask?

"Hmmm." The imaginary prospector stroked his imaginary, yet still filthy, beard. "OK."

Bill was pretty sure the nap was real, even if nothing else was.

But when he woke up, Gabby Gormless and the burro were still there, along with the ashes of the campfire.

"You're a mighty persistent mirage," Bill told him.

"Waall, I reckon I am, at that. You want some cold coffee 'fore I pour it out?"

Bill took a cup. For a hallucination, it was remarkably strong. If it had been real, it would have shocked him out of any hallucinations. Since he could still see Gabby and the burro, the coffee must have been imaginary, too.

They set off down the tunnel, their way lit by a lamp hanging around the burro's neck. It was an electric lamp, but it had been designed to look like an old-fashioned kerosene lamp, down to the flickering, unsteady flame. Gabby whiled away the time by telling incredibly boring and repetitive stories of his adventures and explorations. Bill figured that since he—or his subconscious, which in his case was very nearly the same thing—was inventing these stories himself, he wouldn't miss anything by ignoring them.

There was no real way of measuring time down here on the bottom of the mine, at least not without a watch. Bill couldn't be sure that time passed at the same rate in a hallucination, but they stopped for another illusory meal on the way. Bill was impressed with how well the imaginary inflatable logs burned (there was no other source of wood down here, so Gabby had to carry his fuel with him), and noted how he even felt as though he was getting stronger after each meal, although that was clearly impossible. The coffee was doing the same, and that was even more impossible, considering where it had started. And he had learned to avoid the imaginary muleshit after sitting on a pile.

All in all, it was much more pleasant than stumbling around in the dark and waiting to die. Of course, Bill was still convinced that that was exactly what he was doing, but this version of it was undoubtedly superior. Bill was enjoying the mirage so much that he was shocked and stunned when he suddenly realized he was walking alone and in silence. He gasped as he grasped the meaning of it—that he was probably very close to death now, and would have to go on alone from here. He sobbed, and she pushed a few tears, for his wasted youth, his lost homestead on Phigerinadon IV, his boon companions Sam and Sid, whom he would never see again, and even for the lost companionship of his mirage.

He wept bitterly, Bill did, until at last he heard the sound.

"Psst."

Bill looked up.

"Psst."

There was nothing ahead of him but another of the many intersections in the tunnels.

"Psst."

Bill looked back.

Gabby! He had not vanished after all! Bill leaped up, ran, and embraced the fantastical prospector, so overjoyed was he.

"Tarnation, Bill," Gabby whispered, "get ahold of yerself. An' keep yer yap shut. There may be guards up around that next corner. Wait back here with the burro while I go check it out."

This was becoming an extraordinarily complex mirage. Bill tried to protest that none of this was really necessary, but Gabby shushed him again and strolled up and around the bend. Bill leaned up against the stolid, if nonexistent, burro. It was comforting, since it reminded him of his robomule back on the farm, but it lacked the warm, reassuring smells of metal and lubricants. It smelled instead like a dirty old mule.

After what may or may not have been a long time, Gabby came back.

"Waall, young feller, I had me a piece of luck. One o' my old friends is the assayer in these parts, and he put me in touch with the resistance. They're gonna help you get outa here. How you like them apples?"

"Just fine, sir. I'll take a dozen. So you're going to vanish now?"

"Not exactly, sonny. First you've got to meet your contact. You go up to the intersection, take a left, take the first right, walk exactly one hundred paces, and wait there. When someone says to you, 'The blind fox sleeps at the midnight crossroad,' you say 'But does the midnight crossroad know that the blind fox is sleeping there?' That's yer recognition code. Got it?"

"Sure," Bill said offhandedly. He assumed that anyone this mirage put him in touch with would also be an illusion. How much difference could a code make to a hallucination?

"Fine. Good luck to ya, Bill. Now me and the burro gotta go back to lookin' fer the great neutron mother lode. Burros got a good nose for neutrons, you know. Just like pigs with truffles. See ya around!"

And Gabby and his pack animal plodded slowly off into the tunnel, leaving Bill in the darkness again.

He turned around so as to face the right way, stuck his hands out, so he'd know when he reached the wall, and started off to meet his contact. He found the wall with no trouble, and by keeping his right hand on the wall found the right turn easily enough. Bill got into position and waited.

After a while, a small bobbing light appeared at the far end of the passage. In case this wasn't his contact, Bill tried to look nonchalant. Unfortunately, his supply of nonchalant activities was very limited, and by the time the light got close enough for Bill to see what he was doing, he was on his third round of whistling while buffing his nails on his shirt.

"The blind fox sleeps at the midnight crossroad," said a voice behind the light.

Since the light was in his eyes, Bill couldn't see who was speaking. "The something or other does something," Bill said feebly, wishing he had made some attempt to remember.

"That's not it. Not even close."

"No? How about 'The crossroad slumbers neath the midnight sun?"

"That's not even close. You a spy?"

"No, I'm Bill."

The voice sighed. "That's what Gabby said your name was. You could have made *some* effort at the password, you know."

"I don't remember so good in the dark," was Bill's feeble response.

"Not the world's best excuse. Look, I'm with the Underground. That mean anything to you?"

"We're all underground. It's a mine."

"Come on, Bill. Gabby sent me."

"That's nice."

"Shut up. Just follow me." The light turned and started moving away again.

And so Bill was saved.

## CHAPTER 16

SMUGGLING BILL INTO THE WORKER'S BAR-
racks was almost embarrassingly simple. After all, no
one expected an outsider to sneak into the mine from
deep in the ground. The search for Bill, never very
thorough in the first place, was long over. The soldiers
were long gone. Orders had been left to grab him if he
appeared and shackle him and put him to work in the
mine.

So, whistling with forced casualness, Bill just strolled
into the barracks, traded his incredibly filthy cleansuit
for a fresh one with a number stenciled across the back,
then blended in with the crowd.

There once had been a time, before he had come to
the mine, when Bill would have been recognized, when
people would have surrounded him, asking for autographs and recognition and the magical touch of a celebrity. But now, with a stylish growth of designer
stubble all over his face, no one recognized him.

No one, that is, except two of his barracks-mates.

The Underground Resistance had organized itself

pretty quickly here in the neutron mine. Of course miners have always been well organized, as well as exploited and killed in rock falls and such. With all the new political prisoners checking in right after the coup there was no problem recruiting ringleaders. They realized at once the importance of a real live enemy Trooper and figured out lots of ways that he could be useful to their cause. So in order to protect him they kept his options limited.

Purely for his own good, naturally.

But the resistance saw to it that he didn't talk with anyone they didn't approve first, while nobody even got a good look at him unless they were part of the inner circle.

Nevertheless, there were those two guys that Bill noticed, who kept looking at him from across the barracks. One of them pointed to Bill, and the two spoke for a while, and the first one started over toward Bill, but the Resistance leader who had collected Bill, Commandante Luther Anastasius Lambert Hendricks Bavan Drosophila Melanogaster Farkleheimer, cut them off before they could get within speaking distance, ordered them out of the room. He warned Bill they had to be careful of assassins.

(Commandante Luther Anastasius Lambert Hendricks Bavan Drosophila Melanogaster Farkleheimer was a *nom de guerre*, chosen in order to protect his identity, and also to create as much of a problem as possible for the junta's secretarial staff. He knew that the computers were programmed to accept up to three names with a total of up to thirty letters. Entering his new name, he reasoned, would bring the system to a halt. His friends, however, called him Ed, which was his real name.)

Bill wasn't keeping up much with current events because he was busy being taught all about neutron mining. It was important that on his next shift he should be able to look like he knew what he was doing, so as not to draw too much attention. Commandante Luther Etc. also didn't want Bill to look as though he was too experienced, since that might draw even more attention. Bill told the commandante not to worry because he had always been a slow and careful learner who had even mastered all the complications of fusetending. That is plugging the fuses in and out.

The guard in charge of the neutron face where Bill went to work was probably a slow learner, too. He believed everything he was told, no matter how stupid it sounded, and nodded his head enthusiastically when he was assured that Bill had worked there before. When Bill stood silently for several minutes in front of his assigned machine, scratching his head, the guard accepted that as well.

Which was a good thing. Bill stood and stared at the controls, waiting to remember something, anything, about how the thing worked.

There were two big buttons and a lever. Nothing was labeled clearly; one of the buttons was green and one was red, and there was a big two-headed arrow next to the lever, one head pointing toward Bill and one head pointing away.

Bill studied them. Tentatively, he pushed the lever from the middle position all the way away from him. It clicked into place, but nothing else happened. He pulled it all the way toward him. Again, it clicked; but that was all.

That wasn't it, then.

Bill was developing a real appreciation of the technical skill involved in mining. It was every bit as hard as Technical Fertilizer Operation, which would have been Bill's specialty if he had managed to pursue a career in agriculture.

Bill thought hard, then returned the lever to the middle. It must have been left there for a reason.

Bill thought hard again. He delved deep into his memory, going back yet again to the epochal battle in which he had saved the *Christine Keeler* by carefully directing his weapon away from the green light, and aiming it at the red one. "Red is the one we want to hit," he thought.

He pushed the red button.

Nothing happened.

He'd tried almost everything. This was starting to get frustrating, and besides, the guard was looking over suspiciously. In desperation, Bill pushed the lever forward and pushed the green button.

The machine roared to life and lurched forward, pounding the wall with hundreds of little hammers to loosen the neutron ore. Large robot hands swept the ore to the side and back, leaving a fairly neat pile for the collecting team to sweep up and shovel onto the conveyor belts to the processing room. A third team would follow up with vacuum cleaners to pick up any stray neutrons, which were carefully counted and logged to prevent pilferage.

Bill ran after the hammering machine, which was hammering away from him at a good pace, and grabbed the two huge handles. By pulling and pushing on those, he could keep the crosshairs in the middle of the video screen squarely on the little animated neutron, which was trying to get away from him.

It wasn't quite as easy as using the joystick on the TAIL GUNNER! system, but it was well within Bill's intellectual capacity. In fact, it was a lot like steering a robomule.

Insulated from interruptions (particularly by those two guys from the barracks, who kept trying to get Bill's attention, or according to the commandante, to assassinate him) by Commandante Etc. and his men, Bill lost himself in his work.

Despite the commotion behind him ("No, really, we just want to talk to him. We *have* to talk to him. Of course it's important, but we can't tell you what it's about.") Bill quickly got the hang of it. Or at least enough of the hang of it, he figured, to keep from attracting too much attention for the short time he would—hopefully—be here.

After all, Commandante Etc. and his men were going to smuggle Bill out of the mine so he could rally support for his good buddy, President Millard Grotsky. The generals had reported that the president had resigned because of ill health, but this was so obviously a lie that hardly anyone believed them. All it would take, according to the Resistance leader, would be one impassioned speech by Bill, ideally from the top of a tank, and the coup would collapse in the face of popular support for democracy. Then Bill would be a hero and celebrity again, and maybe even get a cushy government job. He was hoping to become head of the Alcohol Control Board, under the impression that it had something to do with quality testing.

And in the meantime, life was fairly good. The beds were uncomfortable, the air was stale, the food was lousy, the only woman in the place worked seventeen levels up and didn't like Bill anyway, there was nothing to drink, he couldn't do *anything* without permission from the guards, there was no time off and nothing to do in it if there had been, and no one was trying to kill him. Yes, life was fairly good. Meaning he was at least temporarily out of the control of the military.

In fact, Bill was giving some serious thought to making a career as a neutron miner. Since they were to all intents and purposes slaves, neutron miners had excellent job security—comparable to Imperial Troopers but with longer life expectancy. The working conditions were certainly no worse here than aboard the *Heavenly Peace*.

So Bill settled in with unwonted fatalism. He worked hard at his machine until he had learned all its subtleties and intricacies. (Pushing the lever forward moved the machine forward; pulling it back threw it into reverse. To some this may seem easy, but don't knock it until you have tried it.) He was meeting his quota with ease. Although the Underground had sent out an order for everyone to work as slowly as they could as a protest against the coup, Commandante Etc. decided that Bill should go at good speed, so as not to attract too much attention.

The work was about as interesting as almost anything in the Troopers, but after a few days as a miner Bill was actually hoping the two assassins would get through to him, since Commandante Etc. and his inner circle spent all their time plotting and getting into arguments about ideology, and Bill didn't understand either the complexity of their plans or the intricacies of their ideology. All he had for amusement was his work; and talking to the assassins, or fighting them off (and Bill never doubted that a trained Trooper could handle two Eyerackian killers), would be a change of pace.

One afternoon, while Bill was steering his neutron-hammerer down a particularly tricky straightaway, Commandante Etc. sidled up to him, Bill watched carefully. He'd never seen anyone sidle before.

"Pretend I'm not here," the Resistance leader muttered.

"OK," Bill said, and turned back to his machine.

"Ee . . . ant . . . oo . . . ere," Bill heard faintly over the hammering. Following his instructions, he ignored it. There were a lot of other similar noises, and he ignored them, too.

Someone tapped his shoulder. It was the commandante again.

"You got that?"

"Got what?" Bill asked. "I was pretending you weren't here."

"Right." The leader silently counted to ten. "Now pretend I am here."

"That's harder," Bill said. "Since you really are here, in order to pretend you are I first have to convince myself you aren't, which is not at all the same as pretending—"

"Stop!" The commandante raised a hand, and had to try lowering it twice before he could unball his fist and rest his hand on Bill's shoulder. "I'm here. Don't pretend I'm not here, don't pretend I am here. I'm just here. OK?"

"Well, *sure*. That's easy. Why didn't you say that to start with?"

The leader silently counted to twenty this time. "We have a plan to get you out of here."

Bill got excited, but almost immediately got worried again. Out was good, sure, it meant SuperGunge-Burgers and beer and possibly even women, but it also meant bombs falling in all sorts of odd places, like where Bill might happen to be. On the other hand, Commandante Etc. had a look of determination on his face that Bill was used to seeing on officers' faces, a look that said Bill didn't have any choice in the matter. So Bill asked, "What's the plan?"

"There is an unguarded corridor on the processing level, right next to the neutron mill room. With your machine here you can tunnel right up to that corridor, go down it for a mile or so, and dig right into the processing room. Then you climb under the machinery and crawl all the way down to the end of the mill, where the neutrons are crated for transport. Got it so far?"

"Sure," Bill said. "I've seen it. There's enough space under the machinery for loose neutrons to be swept up. It'll be tight, but I can do it."

"We'll have two of our men on crating detail tomorrow. You just climb into one of the neutron containers, and you go out in the next shipment. Home free!" The commandante smiled at his own ingenuity.

Bill nodded. "Pretty good. Have you seen one of the crates?"

"No, not exactly. But I'm told they are built to hold a quantomty of neutrons in each one."

"A quantomty?"

"Billions and billions. So there should be room inside for just one of you, right?"

Bill stooped down and shaped the dimensions of one of the boxes with his hands—about two feet on a side. "I don't think so."

Commandante Etc. frowned. He mimed the sides of a larger box, one almost big enough to take Bill if he were carefully disassembled. "Not this big?"

Bill shook his head.

"Bummer," said the commandante. "OK, no problem. We just have to work out a new plan. Bigger boxes, maybe." He muttered to himself all the way back down the tunnel.

But Commandante Etc's next plan, as brilliant as it would have been, was not to be.

The next morning, at roll call, a foreman with a clipboard walked down the line of workers. Three times, he stopped and pointed. "You," he said, each time. When he had finished his selection, he told Bill and the two presumed assassins, "Come with me."

The three men stepped forward, two of them anxiously, Bill more cautiously. He'd been volunteered before, after all.

"These three men," the foreman said to the assembled work force, "are the only three in the entire mine who have exceeded their work quotas. In recognition of which they are going to get the morning off, have lunch with the mine manager, and have their sentences reduced by six hours."

Commandante Etc. tried to slip close to Bill, to give him some no doubt vitally important message, but a phalanx of armed guards formed up around the three privileged men and marched them off to the elevator.

One of the assassins whispered out of the side of his mouth, "Bill!"

A guard poked him in the ribs with his blaster. "No talking!"

The ride up in the elevator was quiet, but Bill could see the two assassins trying to communicate something to him, or to each other, with facial expressions, he had no idea what.

They marched through the maze of hallways, silent except for the echoing tramp of the guards' boots, which had special noisemakers built into them so they would sound like jackboots on cobblestones, even in a carpeted hallway. Bill stopped paying attention after the fifth turn, and almost walked into the door when the group stopped. He got his hand on the door, just under the large **8** just in time to keep it from stamping on his forehead.

The foreman swung the door open, and the guards prodded the three men inside. "Get washed up, and put on fresh cleansuits. Then follow the robot. Don't try to escape. We'll be around, and anyway there's no way out. See you after lunch."

The squad tromped away, except for the two who had been set to guard the door.

"Greetings, ladies or gentlemen, or whatever sex you may be," said the robot. "If you two will take the room on the left, and Brevet Lance Corporal Bill; you take the room on the right, you have six minutes and thirty-seven seconds before we must leave for lunch." The little machine's legs retracted, and a countdown clock appeared.

"There's no time now, Bill, but we've got to talk," one of the assassins said threateningly.

They dressed and regrouped in the living room of the suite with a full half-minute to spare. Bill came out admiring, albeit with some puzzlement, the neat chevron painted onto the sleeve of his cleansuit. The two assassins came out directly at Bill, and he decked one before the other could say, "Bill, it's us! Don't you recognize us?"

Bill didn't uncock his fist, nor did he loosen his grip on the man's throat. "Sure I recognize you. You two have been trying to assassinate me."

The man said something in a deep, guttural language that Bill didn't understand. He pointed at his neck. Bill loosened his hand a little bit. "No, not assassinate you. We were trying to join you. Bill, don't you know who we are?"

Bill looked carefully at the man he held, then at the one who was slowly picking himself up from the floor. They didn't look anything like anyone he knew, not even like each other. "No," he said, "I don't know you."

"I'm Sid," the one on the right said.

"And I'm Sam," the one on the left said.

"They made us shave off our mustaches."

Bill looked from one to the other and back again. "No, that can't be. You don't look anything like each other." They held up fingers to cover their lower lips, and Bill started to see the resemblance. "But you still can't be them. I know, because Sid is the one on the left and Sam is the one on the right."

Sid and Sam looked at each other, and carefully crossed in front of Bill. "Is that better?" Sam asked.

"Well I'll be bowbed!" Bill said. "My good buddies!"

## CHAPTER 17

BILL AND HIS BOSOM COMPANIONS WERE
marched briskly by the robot—followed by the two
guards with blasters and itchy trigger fingers—through
the complicated hallways, to the elevator, and into an
area that Bill recognized.

Actually, it wasn't the area *per se* that Bill recognized,
since every area in the mine looked pretty much the
same, but the person who was sitting in it. Even the
little holographic man and woman wrestling on her desk
were like a touch of home after the bleakness of the
mines.

"Hi, Sylvia!" he said brightly.

"You again," she countered. "Not dead, then." She
looked up at him to make sure. "Snorri's expecting you
in eight seconds. Get inside." She pointed to the corner,
where the door was sliding open.

"Nice seeing you again," Bill chirped.

Sylvia sniffed and ignored him. Sam and Sid dragged
him into the room with the bench.

"Snorri?" Sam said suspiciously.

"Sure," Sid said sibilantly. "He's a persuasive guy. Or maybe a traitor."

"He's an officer," Bill said. "All officers are the enemy. Don't you guys know anything?"

"GEE, BILL, I DON'T THINK THAT'S FAIR!" The gigantic image of Snorri Yakamoto on the wall-screen leaned forward to adjust the volume. "Maybe in the Troopers, but this is a democracy, you know. Or it was until recently, which is pretty close."

"Traitor!" Sam shouted.

"Collaborator!" Sid sneered.

"Where's our lunch?" Bill asked. "We're supposed to get lunch."

"Bill's right," the director said. "You guys should really have something nutritious to eat. You're going to need your strength for your escape."

A small door in the wall rose up, revealing three trays of piping hot GungeBurgers. Bill grabbed at them and began chomping and drooling, reveling in food that involved chewing. He left it to Sid and Sam to figure out the rest of what Snorri meant.

By the time he came up for air everything seemed to be under control. "I don't suppose you have any beer?"

"No, Bill," Snorri's image said. "Now don't you forget that I'm really not a traitor—no indeed! I just figured that I could help President Grotsky best by staying in my job. And here you are! Gee, it all worked out for the best, didn't it?"

"Looks like it," Sam muttered in sullen agreement.

"So you guys can be on your way in a few minutes. I've got my secret back exit into the garage. Your car is still there, and still has a pass on the windshield. Eat up.

"Meanwhile, Bill, since you have pigged your food already, just mosey through the door for a private chat?"

Another door slid open, making a hole in the wall-screen. It was dark behind the doorway, but Bill had the strong feeling that nothing was going to happen unless he went in there—no escape, no more GungeBurgers, nothing. He went in. The door slid closed behind him, leaving him in darkness just like the bottom of the mine.

"Gee, Bill, long time no see, huh?"

The lights came gradually up, revealing a tiny office set into a raised niche in the wall. If it had been to normal scale, it would have been a good-sized office for a standard human being, but it was scaled for someone seven inches tall, and sure enough, behind the desk was someone exactly that height. A camera in front of the desk led into an advanced image-processing computer with a label that said CHINGER-TO-HUMAN CONVERSION UNIT.

"Bgr!" Bill belched. "What are you doing here?"

"Gee, Bill, you know how hard it is to keep a good Chinger down. Don't you want to sit back and reminisce about all our great times together in training at Camp Leon Trotsky when I was disguised as the toadyish human Eager Beager?"

"No," Bill insinuated.

"Good," Bgr said, relieved. "To tell you the truth, I really hated the Troopers. All that human BO all the time. But I thought even you would have figured out that we Chingers had to be involved here somewhere. I was sent to Eyerack to try to disrupt the war effort and encourage the peace movement here.

"But, gee, it didn't quite work out the way I expected. We Chingers still have so much to learn about war. Killing your own kind—I never would have thought of that one."

"That last foot you gave me—" Bill began.

"Never mind about that now," Bgr said. "You've been a real disappointment to us at the CIA, the Chinger Intelligence Agency. I don't think we can afford to give you any more new feet until we get some real subversion out of you. Besides, that looks like a pretty good foot you've got down there."

Bgr ruminated a moment, then leaned forward and fixed Bill with a baleful stare. "Don't you realize that our entire project here is in your hands? You're the only one who can turn this coup back and restore democracy on Eyerack. Gee, Bill, I thought you liked my pal Millard. So do this for him, if you won't do it for me."

Bill thought about it long and hard.

"Can I have another GungeBurger—and a beer?"

"You got it."

"Then it's a deal." A minute later, after wiping his chin and licking his fingers he belched, "That means I get out of here?"

"You get out."

"Okay. Where's the back door?"

Nothing seemed to have changed much on the surface of Eyerack since the coup. Bombs were still falling more or less at random, more or less everywhere. The roads were still in pretty bad shape. And most of what seminormal life persisted in the face of the Emperor's demonstrations of his loving forgiveness was limited to the underground shopping malls.

The air was generally pretty smoky, and the sun had a little trouble brightening the scene, but it was still a lot more cheery outside—except for the bombs—than in the mine.

Sam and Sid and Bill drove along in their armored car with the top hatch open, enjoying the breeze, basking in the success of their incredibly clever ploy to get past the guards at the entrance to the mine.

"That sure was an incredibly clever ploy, Sam," Bill said. "Could you explain it to me one more time?"

"Gee, Bill, I don't think so," Sam said, looking up from scribbling all over a pile of computer paper. "It was incredibly complicated, as well as being incredibly clever, and you haven't understood it the last eight times I explained it. Let it slide. Take a break. Enjoy the fresh air and sunshine."

Bill shrugged and stood up in the hatch. He took a deep breath of the smoky air, coughed, and sighed. In a few hours they would get to the city that Sam and Sid and Bgr (who the other two still thought was just Snorri) had selected for Bill's dramatic speech against the coup. They would find a tank, Bill would climb up on top and rouse the populace into a democratic frenzy, the generals would be overthrown, peace would reign, and Bill would get a cushy job.

This plan was simple enough for Bill and he thought it was a pretty good plan, with only one problem. He wasn't much good at giving speeches.

The drama part wouldn't be hard. He figured he could handle that; he'd acted in plays when he was in pre-elementary school, and his performance in "The Beast with Ten Fingers" had been reviewed in the school newspaper as "Digitally dramatic." He'd played one of the fingers.

But that role, while it had stretched Bill's talents almost to the limit, hadn't had a lot of lines. Though a lot of scratching was involved. Even his time as an Eye-rackian celebrity hadn't involved much that wasn't ad-libbed. One or two lines at a time, tops.

And now he had a whole speech to do. Bgr had worked with Bill before, and knew that letting Bill improvise a stirring oration was, to be generous, risky. So he had written a speech for Bill, a speech that was practically guaranteed to have the desired effect. All Bill had to do was memorize it.

"Memorize it!" Bill had sputtered, hefting the printout. "I won't even be able to read it before we get there!"

But there was no time to put together either a new speech or a new plan. Their only chance was to have Sam cut the speech down to an hour or two—reduce it to words of one syllable or less—while they were en route, and then feed the high points to Bill one at a time and hope for the best.

So Bill's reverie was interrupted periodically when

Sam passed him another page. Bill read most of them, lost a few in the breeze, and remembered practically nothing. In this way he had more or less mastered the speech to his own satisfaction by the time they reached the central square of Central Square, their destination.

Central Square was a medium-sized city with a medium-sized university. Bgr's studies told him that this was likely to be a hotbed of unrest and dissent, which would catch fire from Bill's speech and spread over the surface of Eyerack, cauterizing the wound of the coup and stretching the metaphor beyond all reasonable limits.

Sid drove their armored car right up to the edge of the plaza. It was evening. There were a few people sitting at an outdoor cafe at one end (since General Weissearse had to lead each wave of the Imperial attack, the Eyerackians had been able to work out the schedule; outdoor dining was popular during the bombing lulls), and a few more milling around near the statue of Gar Ganchua, the city's founder. Most of the people, though, were gathered near a tank that was parked in front of what looked like the city hall.

"Superb," Sam said. "We have an audience waiting for us. Perhaps there's even a protest already in progress."

"Gee, Sam, that doesn't look like a protest to me." Bill shook his head to clear it. *Gee?* Had he said that? He'd been hanging around with the wrong sort for too long. "They look like they're watching something."

"No, it must be a silent vigil against the junta, I'm sure of that. See how they aren't talking to each other? See how they concentrate on the front of the building? They're applying moral force without provoking a violent response. Excellent strategy."

"I'm not entirely sure of that," Sid said thoughtfully. "Shouldn't there be signs or something if it's a vigil?"

"Of course." Sam pointed across the crowd. "And there's a sign. Can you read it?"

They all peered over at the sign, but it was too far away for any of them to make it out.

Trying to be as inconspicuous as possible, they worked their way around to the front of the building and stayed close to the wall while they sidled over toward the tank. Bill hoisted himself up one of the treads and crouched beside the hatch; Sam handed him the final revised copy of the speech.

Making his appearance as dramatic as possible, Bill suddenly stood atop the hatch, facing the silent crowd, his arms thrown wide in greeting.

A tumultuous noise rose from the assembled people, a veritable torrent of sound, all aimed at Bill. He basked in the joy his arrival had caused.

But only for a moment, until he figured out what the people were shouting.

*"Down in front!"*

But he could not be stopped; an evanescent thespian flame burned hotly in his bosom.

*"Get out of the way!"*

"Friends, Eyerackians—" Bill began. He felt a tugging on his pants leg, but went on.

*"Move your bowby body!"* someone yelled, and a few people were shaking their fists now.

Sid was yanking on Bill's leg now. It was time to pay attention.

"Bill! Get down here!" Sam was shouting to be heard over the increasingly angry crowd, and waving at Bill to get off the tank.

"No, I've got their attention now! Let me give the speech!"

Sid finally got enough of a grip in Bill's leg to topple him completely over. The two bodyguards caught him before his head hit the pavement. Some of the crowd cheered, and some booed.

"I don't think this bunch is going to be very receptive, Bill. Look." Sam pointed at the sign they'd seen earlier.

Now they were close enough to read it. "Old-Time

Outdoor 2-D Movie Night," it said. Bill looked behind where he'd been standing. Dim grayish images flickered on the wall. Sid pointed out that everyone in the audience was wearing some kind of headset, no doubt carrying the sound from the "movie," whatever that was.

Bill kicked at a pebble. "OK," he said. Then he cocked his head and raised one finger. "I've got an idea." This was the pose he always saw in the comix when somebody got an idea, and he was still practicing being dramatic.

"No, Bill, I don't think you better have one." Sam shook his head.

"Probably a bad idea," Sid agreed. They started dragging Bill back to the armored car.

Bill stamped his Swiss Army Foot. When the rattling stopped, he said, "But you haven't heard it yet."

"Well, no, not technically."

"But we've heard some other ideas of yours, and if this one is just as good, then maybe we aren't too enthusiastic."

"But we could go to the university!" Bill pleaded.

Sam and Sid stopped in their tracks. They looked at each other.

Sam said, "Hmm."

Sid said, "Indeed."

"Could it be?"

"Law of averages."

"Right. Had to work out. That's actually a good idea, Bill. Let's go."

The main quad at the university was full of activity; so busy, in fact, that hardly anyone noticed when the armored car drove up. There was a tank there, however, and a crowd of people around it, and this crowd wasn't just standing there. They were shouting and yelling and screaming and talking loudly, and some of them were shaking their fists. This was far more promising than the central square.

"How are we doing up there?" one student was asking as Bill and his bodyguards approached the tank.

"One more, I think," said a hollow-sounding voice. Could he have been inside?

Bill vaulted atop the tank's turret, but he couldn't stand on the hatch; it was open. Ever neat, he started to close the hatch, but a head popped up from inside.

"No way, man, you're much too big. We need someone smaller. Maybe one of the girls?"

"What?" Bill inquired.

"You'll never fit inside. We need someone small. If we get one more person in here, we'll break the record for students inside a tank."

Bill looked in. It was pretty crowded in there, all right. It was even worse than a troopship. "No, I don't want to get inside. I'm just here to make a speech."

"Oh. In that case, before you begin, could you bring one of the girls up here?"

Bill hoisted the smallest coed he could find up onto the turret and lowered her feet down the hatch. Another student passed him a beer, and Bill drank it before shouting for attention. He began his speech.

# CHAPTER 18

"YOU MAY ALREADY BE A WINNER!"

The opening of the speech didn't have quite the impact that Bill expected. Bgr had told him that this speech was guaranteed, start to finish. It had been carefully constructed by the Chinger computerized speech-writing program. But there was no shock of recognition electrifying the crowd.

"Friends, Humans, Eyerackians, lend me your sneers. I come to borrow Grotsky, not to raise him!"

A few more people were paying attention now, but they didn't look particularly excited. One of them, following instructions, did sneer though. They must have been a pretty impressionable lot.

"Vice in defense of liberty is no extremism!"

This was supposed to be a rousing speech, but only a few of the students in the quad looked roused at all, and those seemed to be paying more attention to students of the opposite sex than to Bill.

Bill didn't really understand that, but he didn't really understand most of the speech, either. This was not a surprise, all things considered, but it did interfere with his giving the truly brilliant performance he knew was in him.

It couldn't be that the speech was somehow defective. Bgr had explained it all in excruciating detail.

"You see, Bill, the speech is the culmination of extraordinary research and intelligence work by some of Chingerkind's finest minds. MA–5, our crack military archaeology unit, dug up an ancient human memory bank, and reconstructed a large dictionary of quotations. You can imagine how old it was—it still had favorable references to liberty and freedom, and included quotes from people who were not related to the Emperor."

Bill whistled in awe at such inconceivable age.

"We're pretty sure we got the quotations right. So before I had my computer here write the speech, I ran a keyword and subject search on the quotations, looking for victory, freedom, liberty, democracy, and the like, and added the results to the data file. And that means that much of the speech you'll be giving will really have been written by many of humanity's greatest politicians and thinkers and orators. You will be drawing on the deep-seated archetypes that lead humans to altruistic behavior. Do you understand?"

Bill nodded sincerely. "No," he said. Bgr sighed loudly.

"Never mind. Just trust me. We cannot fail!"

Bill had had some considerable experience with human military geniuses, and that experience told him that when they said "Just trust me. We cannot fail!", the wisest course of action was to keep your head as low as possible to prevent its being shot off. His experience with Chinger military geniuses was much more limited; in fact, the only Chinger, military genius or no, he had ever known, was Bgr, and that wasn't much of a sample on which to base vague generalizations. But Bgr sometimes seemed to know what he was talking about. That alone placed him head and shoulders above the human military geniuses.

So Bill had taken Bgr's words at face value.

Now he plowed on through the text, pausing occasionally only long enough to try to get the pages in order or accept another beer. He bellowed parts of it. He whispered other parts of it. He cajoled the audience, and he threatened it. He was eloquent, and he spoke plainly. He emoted his guts out.

Yet, bit by bit, the students drifted away.

The last of them were climbing out of the tank when Bill grabbed one.

"What's going on?" he demanded with a shake.

"Op-op-op-op-sh-sh-sh-sh-ak-ak-ak-i-i-i-i," she said.

He stopped shaking her. "What?"

"I said," she said as he lowered her to the ground, "'Stop shaking me.'" She straightened out her clothes and Bill watched approvingly. "That's better."

"Certainly better than most. But what's going on?"

"Oh," she said, "there's a lecture demonstration on goldfish-swallowing as a deconstruction of alligator-wrestling in the swimming pool at the gym."

"What about my speech?"

"Old. Tired. Irrelevant. What else?"

Sid and Sam helped Bill and the dark-haired young woman down from the tank.

"Irrelevant?" Sam asked, horrified.

"Yeah. As in, nothing to do with the situation, you know?"

"But it was a call to the highest principles, freedom and democracy and all that."

"Yeah. So?" She started toward the gym, and the men followed.

Sam was stumped. Sid stepped in. "Don't you believe in democracy? Don't you believe in President Grotsky?"

"He's probably dead. What's the diff if I believed in him?"

Bill took a turn, "Don't you want to fight the tyranny of the junta?" That phrase came out of the speech. "Do you want the military running *everything*?" That phrase, and the genuine terror it carried, came out of Bill's own experience.

The girl stopped in her tracks. She waited for the three men to find her again, and said, "Look, under the Empire, things were peaceful. Rotten, maybe, but peaceful. Then Grotsky came along, and the Troopers—guys just like you, hotshot," and she poked Bill in his gut with a remarkably strong finger, "—started dropping bombs on us. Students were getting drafted. So under Grotsky we had bombings and the draft, and under the junta we have bombings and the draft. What's the difference?"

"Is that how everyone feels?" Sam asked.

"Pretty much," she said.

"All the students?" She nodded. "You've all talked about it?"

"Of course. That's what we do. We're students. What did you think we're in college for?"

Bill thought it over. "For the parties?"

"Okay, yeah, but in between parties we talk."

This was a possibility that Bill and Sam and Sid had never considered. For Bill the new idea was that people did something besides enjoy heterosexuality and drink at college. Since all of his knowledge of higher education was gleaned from the comix this was understandable. But Sam and Sid were horrified that no one seemed to care that their beloved President Grotsky was being held captive by the military high command. The bodyguards muttered darkly to each other about this while the group proceeded toward the lecture demonstration.

Bill, meanwhile, was trying to convince Calyfigia, for that was indeed the coed's name, that he was the moral equivalent of a student and thus eligible for the party perks that went with being in college. She wasn't buying any of it, but that didn't deter Bill in the slightest.

He was concentrating fully on this project when his

erstwhile bodyguards interrupted him.

"Bill, we've made a decision."

"Sure guys, whatever. Just give me a few minutes, Okay?"

"Bill, we're leaving."

"Why?"

"We owe Millard too much to let him rot in some jail. We're going to take the armored car and find him and rescue him so we can restore democracy."

"Sure, great. Good luck," Bill enthused with complete indifference, his eyes fixed on Calyfigia's most attractive bottom.

Sid scuffed one shoe back and forth on the pavement. "We wouldn't object if you decided to come with us."

Bill looked at them, and at Calyfigia, and back again. On one side, a grand moral enterprise. On the other side, a remote chance at immoral behavior. On one side, the certainty of good company and adventure, and the possibility of glory. On the other side, almost certain humiliation and failure.

It was the "almost" that was decisive.

"If it's all right with you guys I think that I'll stay right here. It's time I got myself an education, think of the future . . ."

This flood of insincerity was interrupted by the sound of exploding bombs. The afternoon attack had begun.

Some of them were exploding quite close to Bill and Calyfigia as they waved goodbye to the fleeing Sam and Sid.

*Kaboom!*

"That was the math building," Calyfigia said. She checked her watch. "There isn't even supposed to be an attack now! Those bowby Trooper buddies of yours have changed the schedule again."

Bill tried to explain that despite his uniform the Troopers, and particularly the people who made up the attack schedules, were no buddies of his, except in the most technical sense, but Calyfigia didn't listen.

"We've got to get to a shelter. The one under the math building's probably no good." She looked around to see which one might be closest.

*Kaboom!*

"Athletic dorm," Calyfigia said absently.

Bill noted that the athletic dorm had been a lot closer to where they were standing than the math building had been.

"Geology building!" Calyfigia said emphatically.

"I didn't hear the kaboom," Bill said.

"No, that's where the nearest shelter is. Follow me."

Calyfigia already understood the zig-zag run that Bill had had to teach Sam and Sid, and she used it even though nothing was falling out of the sky directly at them. Bill admired the professionalism of that. He also followed it closely.

He was following so closely that he was able to hear the bomb coming and throw Calyfigia to the ground just before the geology building blew up.

Buildings, even the ones with shelters, didn't seem to be a very good bet for survival.

Bill and Calyfigia stayed where they were for a while, trying to become one with the ground. Bill also made a few tentative attempts to become one with Calyfigia, but with all those little bits of ground and bomb and building and who knew what else flying around, his heart wasn't really in it.

Eventually, the attack wave passed over them and the bombs stopped falling and the ground stopped shaking. Bill stopped shaking not long after, and stood up to find Calyfigia already brushing herself off.

"I guess the semester's over," she said.

"Huh?"

"Look around."

Bill did that. She was right. School was out for the duration, unless they wanted to hold classes outdoors. And live in tents. Parts of a few buildings were still standing, and most of the stadium, but basically the campus was ready for planting. Beyond the campus there was more rubble, and even a few buildings standing. People were already picking through the rubble, looking for friends or possessions or anything that might still be in a usable condition.

A line of people was threading across the campus, heading for what remained of the highway that led into the countryside.

Central Square was being abandoned.

*CHAPTER* **19**

BY THE TIME THEY HAD SALVAGED WHAT
they could of Calyfigia's belongings from her dorm
room (a pencil, a lace nightie, three pairs of socks, and
a lead-weighted cosh) and joined the stream of refugees,
the road was so crowded that even those with working
vehicles were moving at a walking pace.

Bill had offered to help carry Calyfigia's things, but
she rightly suspected that he just wanted to handle her
lingerie, and besides, there was room for it all in her
pockets. Bill's own few possessions had gone off in the
armored car with Sam and Sid, but he was used to
traveling light.

He was also used to marching, and being able to do
it without the standard Imperial hundred-pound pack (a
supply of stones was kept in most barracks, in case the
men had trouble getting their packs up to weight) was
almost a pleasure.

In fact, as he got into the rhythm of it, he did start
enjoying himself. There was an attractive woman at his
side, and even if she didn't like him much she hadn't

hit him with the cosh yet. The weather was good—sunny with moderate smoke and intermittent shrapnel, along with a seventy percent chance of heavy bombing toward evening—and his boot (an Eyerackian replica of Trooper issue made to Bill's description) was comfortable.

So he was a little surprised by Calyfigia's foul mood. Sure, her home had been blown up, her school had ceased to exist, everything she owned had been destroyed, and many of her friends were dead or missing, but Bill knew that you could get used to all these things. They had happened to him plenty of times. He tried to cheer her up by pointing out that (a) they were still alive, and (b) they were likely to stay that way for at least the next few hours. But even that didn't didn't seem quite to do the trick.

Finally she exploded. "This is all your fault, you know!"

Bill was flabbergasted. "Me? What did I do?" he flabbergasted.

Calyfigia stabbed her finger into his stomach. "This is a uniform, isn't it? You're a soldier, aren't you?"

"Sure, but I'm not one of *your* soldiers."

She looked at him and his uniform carefully. "I've seen you somewhere before, haven't I?"

Patiently, he explained. "I was the guy standing on the tank back on the quad, when there was a quad. I gave a speech. You remember, don't you?"

"Not that, you military moron, before that. Not one of ours. That's an Imperial Trooper uniform, isn't it?"

With a certain reluctance he admitted as how it was (although again, it was slightly modified, since the Eyerackian tailors had made it from his description, out of real cloth instead of recycled paper).

She took a good look at his Swiss Army Foot, which was indeed pretty distinctive even in this crowd. "You're Bill, aren't you?"

"Sure. Didn't I introduce myself?" He stuck his hand out.

She ignored it. "You're the celebrity prisoner of war, right?"

Bill looked around nervously. "Actually, right now I'm the celebrity escaped prisoner of war. That's why I've kept this beard."

"So this is all your fault!" She glared at him and made a sweeping gesture that included the refugees, the bombing, the war, the coup, and her former holorecord collection.

Bill considered for a moment whether he should take the credit, but not only wouldn't that be honest, but he was beginning to get a sneaky notion that this would not make much of an impression on Calyfigia. "Actually, none of it was my idea," he sniveled, wallowing in self-pity. "You could even say I was opposed to it, although not in front of an officer. That's not the Trooper's way."

"And you're a Trooper through and through. You're a cog in the war machine!"

"Is that bad?"

It was Calyfigia's turn to be flabbergasted. She was so upset that she couldn't talk for another mile or so.

Bill didn't quite understand what she was getting at, although he sort of liked her company a lot more when she wasn't talking. He'd been a Trooper for so long, and had been so thoroughly indoctrinated, that even though he hated being a Trooper he couldn't see himself in any other kind of life. He was Bill, Trooper. It was more like an equation than a name: Bill = Trooper.

But later, when he was helping an old woman haul her shopping cart out of a bomb crater, Calyfigia spoke again. "You're just a hired killer!" she said.

The old woman looked at him with alarm. "But not you," he explained. "That means that the people who hired me last didn't order any killing. Yet."

"Hah!" Calyfigia said.

"No, really," Bill whimpered. "Killing people isn't fun." He thought a moment. "I mean it can be satisfying, especially when they're trying to kill me. Except for officers, I never kill anyone for fun, and even that is really self-defense."

"You could have resisted."

"Resisted?" It was a shocking thought, one that had never occurred to Bill before. "How?"

"You didn't have to enlist."

"I was drafted." This wasn't strictly true, although Bill considered it morally true. Technically, there was no draft in the Empire, and Bill *had* signed the voluntary enlistment papers. Of course, he had been under the influence of hypnotic and ego-dissolving drugs at the time, and had no memory of signing the papers, but he had seen them, and that was his signature all right. But it hadn't been his idea, so he considered it the same as being drafted.

None of that mattered to Calyfigia, even if he'd explained it. "That is a feeble excuse," she sneered. "You could have fled. Snuck over the border at night to avoid being drafted."

"What border? The whole planet belonged to the Emperor."

"Then, you could have resisted from inside the Troopers. But, oh no, you're a Galactic Hero, right? You should have been working for peace, trying to end wars instead of waging them. Why should you be loyal to people who leave you with a foot like that, and those ridiculous fangs?"

Bill stopped and looked at his foot. He liked this one pretty well; it was a lot better than some of the feet he'd had on his right leg. It wasn't as good as a real human foot, but it did a lot of things a real foot couldn't. And he'd gone to a lot of trouble to get those fangs. He didn't think they were ridiculous at all. This girl was being highly unreasonable.

He tried to explain how he had tried to work with

Bgr the Chinger to promote peace, but he couldn't make any of his failed, half-hearted exploits sound very good, and he was a little uneasy bragging about what was, after all, treason.

Fortunately, he was interrupted by a new attack from the sky.

General Weissearse must have been seeing old war holos, because this attack began with a strafing run down the middle of the road. At the speed of an Imperial fighter, the bullets were coming down at about one every fifty yards, so most of them didn't hit anything, but the crowd was really panicked by the noise. They fled in all directions.

Bill took a quick look at the sky and saw that the first fighter had already passed—but another was heading their way. He shifted into drill instructor mode.

"GET OFF THE ROAD AND GET DOWN!" His voice boomed over the noise of the mob, and people started obeying like recruits—without any questions. He had to repeat the order a couple of times, but by the time the second fighter made its run, no one was standing in the middle of the road any more except Bill and Calyfigia.

He was watching the sky to see how the attack might develop. She was castigating him for ordering people around.

But the fighter was coming back. Bill pushed her aside and dived after her. She tumbled over a few times before landing in one of the conveniently placed bomb craters. He arrived an instant later. A slug whipped through the space where she'd been standing.

Bill climbed back onto the road, warning everyone else to stay as low as they could get. A third fighter was beginning its run.

He looked up and down the road. There were two bodies within a couple of hundred yards of him. He ran to the nearest. It was a small boy, not injured but too scared to move. Bill picked him up and threw him toward a crowd in a crater. "Catch!" he yelled.

Bill pounded down the broken highway toward the second body, looking back over his shoulder to keep track of the fighter. At most he only had a few seconds. His trained reflex when he saw the man was to call for a medic, but then he realized that there was no medic; there was no one but himself. It was only a flesh wound in the leg, but it had to be painful for the guy when Bill grabbed him and rolled them both over to the side of the road. The third fighter passed by, and Bill took a moment to tear off one sleeve of the man's shirt and tie it over the wound. He carried the man to safety, then went back for Calyfigia.

She was just climbing out of her crater. And she was just getting warmed up. "You've got a lot of gall, treating me like that—"

Bill shoved her back down and jumped in after. He landed right on top of her in the cramped space, knocking the breath out of her so she missed the fourth and final strafing run. He jumped up and out before she could start scolding him again.

Three of the fighters had gone on to more interesting targets with higher point values, but one of them was looping around for another attack.

Bill looked over the remains of the highway. There were no targets left for a strafing attack, except a couple of hovercars that hadn't run off the side. He knew that if *he* had been flying the fighter, a couple of abandoned cars weren't worth enough points to make the run worthwhile. In TAIL GUNNER! they wouldn't have been worth any points at all.

The pilot must have something else in mind.

"EVERYBODY STAY DOWN! THEY HAVEN'T FINISHED YET!" he shouted.

Naturally, Calyfigia was climbing back out of the crater. He tuned out what she was saying, something about his being an uneducated warmongering clod.

Bill didn't have much education and was mostly immune to instruction, but despite himself he had learned something about weapons systems in his years in the Troopers. He was trying to figure out which one the pilot would be likely to use against a bunch of scattered people.

"Hotbody," he said.

"Well, yes, people have told me so, but it's none of your business, and don't change the subject. You have to raise your political consciousness, and understand your place in the war machine—"

"The Hotbody," he interrupted, "is a multiple-warhead self-guiding heat-seeking missile. That's what I'd use if I was him."

"'If I *were* him,' you mean," Calyfigia corrected. The meaning of what he'd said sank in. "What do you mean?"

Bill started looking around for something he could use for defense. "I mean that it's a whole mess of little missiles that will be attracted by people's body heat." There was nothing here except the hovercars—could he use their motors? no, they were all electric jobs—and a few wooden carts. "If you don't get down and stay down you're finished." He looked straight at her and growled, baring his fangs. "Got that?" She bulged her eyes and nodded. "Now leave this to the expert."

He glanced at the fighter. It hadn't fired anything yet. He ran to the nearest cart and dragged it out into the middle of the highway. Then he ran for another.

Bill managed to gather three carts before the two little dots separated from the larger dot of the fighter. He patted all his pockets, but he'd never taken up smoking, so he had no matches, not even in any of the secret compartments in his Swiss Army Foot.

Bingo! He hoisted his foot up, aimed the laser at the wood, and pressed the activator button. A condom popped out of its dispenser. Bill absently picked it up and stuck it in his shirt pocket. He pressed the button for the flame thrower. The bottle opener came out. He pushed it back in. He pulled the lever for the camp stove. The little magnifying glass popped out.

Bill grabbed the magnifier and held it a couple of inches from the nearest chunk of wood. He got the focus, held it and started blowing on the hot spot.

The two little dots were getting bigger and starting to spread out into clouds.

The wood started to smoke. Still holding the magnifying glass, Bill started puffing away, blowing for his life to get a flame.

And there it was at last!

Too dizzy to walk, Bill crawled in a direction he hoped was away from the fire. He made it a couple of yards before the two clouds of missiles gathered into the fire and blew themselves up, and him unconscious.

Bill woke up lying on something soft. He hadn't had too much experience of that lately, so he just stayed where he was, with his eyes closed.

He sighed, and gently flexed the various parts of his body that could have been damaged in the explosion. They all seemed to be there, and mostly undamaged. He moved his head a little bit, from side to side. It was still there, too, and as whole as it ever was.

But it was resting on something soft, and firm, and warm. Something that probably wasn't a pillow.

"You're awake?" It sounded like Calyfigia's voice, but it was soft, and friendly, and warm. Just like the thing that probably wasn't a pillow.

He came a little further awake.

Despite what might have seemed limitations on Bill's intellect, there were two circumstances in which he almost always became fully conscious. In combat, Bill had been hypno-trained to do anything needed to stay alive.

Bill was not so much of an expert in the other circumstance, but it did always get his full attention if he could retain his grip on consciousness at all.

"I'm awake," he said.

The other circumstance, of course, was the prospect of intimate contact with a person of the female gender.

He opened his eyes. He was in the back seat of a luxury hovercar.

"The others explained to me what you did. I'd like to apologize for what I said to you. I had you all wrong."

He looked up. Yes, that dark hair framing a pale face was Calyfigia all right. He wondered if she still had the lace nightie.

"Is there anything I can do," she went on, "to make it up to you?"

Bill opened his mouth, started to speak, but she pressed a warm and gentle finger to his lips.

"No," she husked. "Let's see if I can guess what it will be."

## *CHAPTER* **20**

BILL LEANED BACK IN THE PASSENGER SEAT of the hovercar. It was the only sort of vehicle that could negotiate the roads in their current state. The solar panels on the roof meant they didn't have to worry about finding fuel. Aside from a small problem going uphill—the constant smoky haze in the sky cut down on their power—it was sure a lovely way to travel.

Even hills weren't much of a problem, since they weren't going anyplace in particular.

The grateful crowd on the road had insisted that Bill and Calyfigia take the hovercar, and its owner, his arm well-twisted, had eventually, if grudgingly, agreed.

The car was really well equipped. The seats flipped back to make a lovely bed-like surface, there was air conditioning, auto-pilot, stereo and holovision, microwave oven, autobar, toilet, and Super Nintari GameDwarf system.

If he could only find a place to park away from the others—and find the seat-collapsing button—Bill would be in heaven. As it was, he drowned his frustrations in luxury while they kept steady pace with the other refugees.

Bill took a sip of his drink. The autobar had actually run out of alcohol by the first evening—the original owner and his friends had been raiding it pretty heavily—and now Bill was trying to develop a taste for beet daiquiris while the internal still whipped up a new supply. Beet daiquiris took a lot of getting used to, especially when made without rum, and Bill wasn't making a lot of progress.

In fact, he was bored. At first he'd enjoyed the feeling. He hadn't had much time to be bored since he'd become a trooper, and being bored was kind of interesting at first. But it soon got boring.

And Calyfigia didn't help much. She was a college student, and he had thought that would be exciting, but what it really meant was that as long as the others were there his libidinous ambitions had to be muzzled. So without alcohol or sex to occupy them she fell back on the college student's third interest. She talked about talking about ideas.

Now, Bill had had a number of ideas in his time. Most of them had involved ways of staying alive or getting a drink or a woman. But Calyfigia's ideas were completely unlike those ideas. Calyfigia's idea of a good idea was, "Let's consider Antonin Artaud's idea of the theater as pock de gibble pa kwoz." Or at any rate, that's how it sounded to Bill, who had learned to stop listening when certain names came up in the conversation.

So he leaned back, sipped his alcohol-free beet daiquiri, and very quickly learned how to say "Very interesting" in his sleep.

Still, no one was trying to kill him, and there was always the chance they would find a place to park, and there were still plenty of lima beans and Brussels sprouts in the freezer, so they wouldn't starve. And he was catching up on his sleep.

Bill drifted off, dreaming of his youth on the farm, those carefree days when he would work from dawn to dusk shoveling manure or following his robomule down the furrows breaking clods and collecting stones. He heard once more his dear, sweet mother's voice calling him, felt once more the maternal cattle prod in the side with which she used to wake him. "Get up, bowb-breath."

"Aww, Ma, do I have to?"

"Am I boring you, teensy-brain?"

"Aww, Ma—" Why was his mother talking like that?

Bill shook himself awake. Eyerack. Calyfigia. Right. He looked out the window and saw the entrance to an underground mall. He stretched once, then opened the door and stepped out, scanning the sky for warships. There were only a couple, and not coming this way.

Before he closed the door, Calyfigia stopped him. "Bill, are you bored?" He admitted as how he was. "As bored as I am?"

"Probably more."

"Then you'll understand." She pulled him down and gave him a memorable kiss on the lips. "I'm going to visit my folks."

She slammed the door, and the hovercar took off in a cloud of dust.

Bill looked around.

He was all alone in an empty parking lot, with an entrance to a mall that did him no good, since he had no money. There was a road at the exit. He took it.

Bill tried strolling down the road, but he had been too well trained. Marching was in his blood now, even if he'd had the hypno-coils left out of these boots. And he had to admit that marching covered ground faster than strolling. He wasn't going anywhere in particular, but he'd get there a lot quicker by marching.

Marching had one other advantage. He had done enough of it by now that he could, quite literally, march in his sleep. As long as the road was fairly straight. This road was perfectly straight, as far as he could see it, which was a few miles farther on where it ran into some trees.

Unfortunately, whenever Bill slept while he was marching he always dreamed that he was marching, so it wasn't quite as restful as it might have been. He dreamed that he was marching across a featureless plain toward a small grove of trees. The dream was as featureless as the plain until he reached the grove, and then a voice from the heavens ordered a halt.

Bill awoke to find himself standing in a small grove of trees. He was still on the road, and the road was still straight, but something had stopped him.

There was a smoking pile of wreckage a mile or so away, the remains of an Imperial one-man scout ship, by the looks of it, but that wouldn't have made him stop. He had sleepmarched through fire-fights before; a mere aircraft crash wouldn't have affected him.

"Eyes up!" came an order from the heavens. Bill obeyed.

Hanging in a tree, twenty feet up, was an Imperial Trooper.

"Hi, there," Bill said.

"Hi yourself," the trooper said.

Bill looked from the trooper to the wreckage and back. "That your scout?"

"Yeah. I tried to ride it in, but I had to bail out at the last second."

"Anything worth salvaging on board?"

"I doubt it," the pilot said. "It hit pretty hard."

"Oh. Too bad." Bill started marching again.

"Hey! Wait!"

Bill stopped again. "What for?"

"I'm stuck up here."

"So?"

"Aren't you going to help me get down?"

Bill thought it over. "No."

"Isn't that a Trooper uniform you're wearing?"

"Yeah. So what?"

"So you should help me."

Bill laughed at the idea.

"What is this," the pilot asked, "bowb your buddy week?"

Bill shrugged. "In the Troopers, it's always bowb your buddy week."

"True enough," the pilot admitted. "Suppose I pay you?"

"That's a different story. What've you got?"

The pilot emptied his pockets. "Forty-seven credits."

"Imperial credits?"

"Of course!"

"They're no good here. What else you got?"

The pilot thought for a while. "My survival kit."

"I'm surviving without it. No thanks."

"Wait! It isn't like the grunt's survival kit. Pilots get special treatment, almost like officers."

Bill's interest rose. "What's in it?"

"Let's see. Mess kit, rations, compass, signal flare, suicide pill, medicinal brandy, toilet paper, candy bar, skateboard, stockings, condoms—"

"Hold it a second." It was too late for the condoms, even if these didn't come in the indestructible foil packets, but there was something else on that list. "How big is the bottle of brandy?"

"A fifth. A full bottle."

Bill moved under the pilot. "Drop it down."

The whole survival kit came down, and Bill put it all aside except the brandy. After a moment's thought he took the skateboard, too. Then he examined the situation.

The pilot was hanging by two strands of parachute cord. He could cut them, but the fall would probably break his legs. What he needed was something to cushion his fall.

"Let me gather some branches," Bill said. "I'll pile

them up, then you can cut yourself free and drop into that."

The pilot agreed, and Bill went looking for fallen brush. But there wasn't much, and what was there was mostly old and hard. Bill would need to cut something fresh.

Bill sat on the ground and examined his Swiss Army Foot carefully. Somewhere here, he remembered, was a wood saw. He'd never had any use for it before, but it had seemed like a neat feature when he got the foot. It took a while, but he finally found the button that was marked, in tiny little letters, "wood saw." He pressed it.

The laser flared into life. "Close enough," Bill said to himself. Aiming his foot carefully, he cut most of the branches off the tree that held the pilot. He gathered them up into a pile about five feet high, then remembered to turn off the laser before he cut down any more trees or set any more fires.

The pilot dropped safely down and they introduced themselves.

"Colon? That's a funny name," Bill said.

"My father's interest was punctuation," Colon explained. "My sister is Ampersand."

In the distance they could hear a siren.

"Uh-oh," Bill said. "Forest fire patrol, I'll bet. There's a mall down that way," he pointed in the direction he'd come from, "and you could lose yourself in the crowd if you don't want to get picked up. I'll go the other way, and they'll only get one of us. Okay?"

As soon as Colon was well off toward the mall, Bill cut all the insignia off his uniform, hopped on the skateboard, and went on his way. The military fire trucks passed him without a pause.

Bill soon mastered the art of riding a skateboard, at least in a straight line, and managed to cover even more ground than he could in marching. It was a lot harder to skate and sleep than to march and sleep, but it was interesting enough so that he didn't really need to sleep through it. By the time he started getting hungry, he had entered a shallow valley that opened up into farmland.

A deep breath brought him the heady aroma of fermenting animal manure, so redolent of everything that meant "home." Off in the distance a young man, not unlike Bill himself in his years of childhood innocence, followed his robomule around a field, carving fresh furrows.

Bill hadn't been on a farm since he left home, unless you counted the hydroponic okra plantation on the *Bounty*, and Bill would rather not remember that particular episode, thank you. This might be the perfect place to hide out for a while. He could do chores, eat real food, sleep in a real bed with a real straw mattress, and pretend he wasn't a Trooper. After a while maybe he'd even begin to believe it. It was a heady prospect, all of it raised by the aromas that arose from the nearby mound of porcuswine manure. Each one to his own taste.

With the insignia gone from his uniform, Bill knew he would have no trouble passing himself off as an itinerant skateboarding unskilled laborer; it didn't involve any pretense. All he had to do was find a likely-looking farmstead, preferably one with a good-looking daughter in the front yard, stop the skateboard, and introduce himself.

He coasted down the road into the valley, slowly gaining speed, keeping on the lookout for a house that caught his fancy. He noted that the road was still smooth here, a good sign that this region had somehow avoided Stormy Wormy Weissearse's attentions. Farms didn't make good targets anyway, being all spread out. It took a lot of bombs to destroy even one farm. Of course, General Weissearse had a lot of bombs at his disposal, but surely he had better things to do with them.

Up ahead, on the other side of the road, Bill spotted

a likely house. It was white and well maintained, with a recently whitewashed picket fence enclosing the yard. Roses climbed a trellis at the side of the house, and a few ducks scurried for grubs. A clothesline stretched from the house to the majestic maple at the corner of the property, and a beautiful young woman, her long flame-red hair and prim light blue house dress drifting in the breeze, was hanging an interesting assortment of freshly laundered wholesome female underwear.

Still coasting down the long hill, Bill swerved over to the far side of the road, closing in on his target house. As he came up almost to the corner of the fence, he realized he had omitted one item from his calculations: he didn't know how to stop the skateboard.

It seemed as though it should be simple enough. He put his boot to the pavement as a brake, but he was moving too fast. What seemed like half the sole scraped away, without slowing him down nearly enough. Without a replacement handy, he didn't dare risk the Swiss Army Foot in such a maneuver.

This shouldn't be too hard; he'd done it any number of times in the video arcade, and even if that way involved a joystick and a couple of buttons, and he didn't have any of those available, the basic theory was the same, wasn't it?

He leaned all the way back, raising the front wheels of the board off the ground. The tail went down, pushing against the road. The board stopped on the spot.

Bill, however, had considerable momentum stored up. He proceeded in a gentle arc up and forward, landing shortly thereafter with an impact that, familiarly, knocked him cold.

## *CHAPTER* **21**

IT WAS BY NOW AN ALMOST REASSURING sensation. Not for the first time Bill swam slowly up out of the black pool of unconsciousness; doing the backstroke.

Once again he tested the important parts of his body, finding none of them broken, although there were a few new bruises. Not bad, all things considered.

Once again, before he opened his eyes he tried to get a sense of his surroundings, and once again it definitely seemed as though his head was in somebody's lap. Unless he missed his guess, that somebody had a supple waist, long legs, and long red hair.

This wasn't exactly how he'd planned it, but it couldn't have worked out better. Now he'd have sympathy in his favor, as well as usefulness. Maybe he'd have to spend a day or two in bed before he could start working; that would be nice, being cared for by this angel.

Sensing his slight motion, the woman asked, "Are you awake? Are you all right?" Her voice was musical, the perfect voice for a beautiful woman.

"Oh, I'm fine," Bill said, his plan to play invalid dissipating into thin air. He could never lie to that voice.

"Are you sure?"

"Yes, I'm sure. Just a few bruises. Nothing serious."

She stroked his hair gently for a little while. "What were you doing out there? I've never seen you in these parts before."

"Actually, I was looking for a job. I've done farm work before."

"Wonderful!" The delight in her voice was like cold beer in the summertime to Bill. "So many of our men have gone into the military, good workmen are always welcome. Would you be willing to work for me? I can't pay much, but I can feed you and give you a room. The one upstairs, next to mine, is comfortable. Would you like that?"

Bill smiled. "I would like that very much," he said.

"You promise you won't be lured away to any of the other farms?"

"I promise."

Bill opened his eyes to gaze at the face to which he had just promised. Something seemed wrong with it. Partly, of course, it was the angle; with his head in her lap, he was seeing her upside down. But there was something else; the face reminded him of someone else he used to know, and it wasn't quite the shade of red he had seen from the road. In fact, it was more of a mouse brown. And then he remembered who the woman looked like: his most faithful childhood companion, his confidant, his friend, his robomule.

*Something has gone terribly wrong*, he thought.

He struggled upright to look at the woman right side up. She didn't look much better.

"If you're feeling better," she said in that gorgeous voice, "I should introduce myself. I'm Mrs. Augeas. But we're going to be friends, I can tell. You call me Eunice." She stuck her hand out and Bill introduced himself and shook it, barely escaping serious injury. This was a strong woman. "Let's get you upstairs and settled in, Bill." She smiled invitingly.

Once they were both standing, and particularly while Bill was following Eunice up the stairs, Bill had ample opportunity to assess his situation. Eunice was not much more than ten years older than Bill. She was about the same size Bill was, and while she wasn't quite as broad as he was in the shoulder, she made up for it in the hips. She was certainly a pleasant woman, but not the creature of romantic fantasy that he'd seen from the road. Besides, she'd introduced herself as *Mrs.*, which was, in Bill's experience, usually a pretty good indication that she was married.

"I think my husband's overalls will fit you, Bill," she said, opening a closet in Bill's new room, and they did, once he rolled up the cuffs a couple of times.

Well, all this it wasn't exactly what Bill had had in mind. But it was farm work, and there were no bombs dropping, and the baking smells from the kitchen reminded him of home (his Mom had had the very same OdoRecord of fresh apple pie playing in the kitchen whenever she made Limburger-liver-and-sardine stew, which was on Wednesdays). With a reluctant sigh he set himself to cleaning the piggery. It hadn't been mucked out for a long time—years, at Bill's best guess. He thought about just flooding the place with water, but the hose didn't have enough pressure. It would have to be shovel and barrow.

But hard work was nothing new to Bill, nor the cheerful smell of porcuswine manure. He set to with a will, and by dinner time, although he was not that attractive, one small corner of the barn was gleaming clean.

Over a heaping serving of fried porcuswine rinds, he couldn't help comparing Eunice's place with the redhead's. Each seemed to be run by a woman alone, but one was spick and span, and the other was definitely showing signs of wear and tear. Eunice clearly worked

hard to keep her farm running, and the redhead definitely looked like she had time to keep her skin smooth.
Bill had to ask about her.

"Oh, that's my neighbor, Melissa Nafka. You must
have slid right past her place on your skateboard. An
honest boy like you doesn't want to work for her, oh
no."

"Really?" Bill feigned no more than academic interest.
"She looked so . . . pleasant."

"Well, let me *tell* you. She doesn't lift a finger around
that place. It's a regular scandal, it is."

"It looks pretty well kept up."

"Oh, yes, it is, but not by her, you know. Every man
in the valley is always running over there to do her
chores. No, you wouldn't want to be working for her.
She doesn't pay any of them a single credit for all their
work. An honest boy like you wouldn't have any truck
with her sort."

Bill considered it while he ground down one of the
porcuswine rinds. "Then why do they do it, if she
doesn't pay them?"

Eunice leaned forward as though someone outside
might overhear. "I hate to speak ill of someone behind
her back, as it were, but let me tell you." Her voice
dropped to a whisper. "She *sleeps* with them," she sus-
surated silently, then leaned back and her voice returned
to normal. "Every one of them. Isn't that awful?"

"Absolutely," Bill said hollowly.

Somehow, Bill kept up his end of the conversation
through the rest of the meal, but his heart wasn't in it.
His mind wasn't in it, either, but fortunately he'd made
enough of an impression on Eunice that she didn't expect
brilliance. But Bill was trying to solve a problem.

On the one hand, he'd promised Eunice that he would
work for her, and a promise was a promise. But on the
other hand, if he could finish cleaning the barn tomorrow morning; he could sneak next door in the afternoon.
But on the other hand, it would take weeks to finish

the piggery. And on the last hand, he didn't have that many hands.

The problem still bothered him that night when he went to sleep, and in the morning when he got up. He shaved and put on clean overalls in case the solution to his problem suddenly manifested itself. But even puzzling over it all morning—aided by the friendly presence of the porcuswine—didn't help. Nothing happened right up until the moment he heard the sonic boom.

It was a sound that surely didn't fit in this quiet, old-fashioned valley, where the most difficult concern should have been how to get on line with the amiable redhead. Bill came out of the piggery to see what the boom might token, and he reached the yard just in time to hear the *foom* that followed it.

Snow? Couldn't be; it was the wrong time of year for it on this part of Eyerack. But something was definitely falling out of the sky, something that was coming down much too slowly to be rain or hail or shrapnel or any of the normal weather. And although it was coming down all over the valley, it was coming from five or six specific spots.

Propaganda bombs, Bill realized as he picked one of the leaflets out of the air and read it. YOUR EMPEROR LOVES YOU!, it began. They almost all began that way.

### YOUR EMPEROR LOVES YOU!

"Yes, I do, I really do!"—The Emperor

From the very beginning of our glorious Empire, farmers have represented the very best that the Empire has to offer—strong, devoted, productive citizens who love their Emperor as much as he loves them. Every Emperor has always stayed in close touch with the soil and with those who work it; every Emperor has always owned farmers, and has taken good care of them.

Without farmers, a large part of our food supply

would be disrupted, and several of the Official Imperial Food Groups would be very hard to find. Farmers are very important to the health of the people of the Empire, and that is another reason for your Emperor's special love for all farmers.

Farmers are especially important for armies, because armies eat a lot of food, and produce hardly any. Your Emperor loves armies, so that is another reason for him to love farmers even more.

Sadly, your Emperor's love is not without limit. As much as he loves you, he needs to bring you back into his loving embrace. And in order to do that, he must defeat the foolishly misled armies that, in their obstinate ignorance, resist his love. And the food that you, in dutiful obedience to your traditional role, are providing to the armed forces of Eyerack, is a dagger in the heart of your Emperor. The longer the armed forces of Eyerack resist, the greater destruction your Emperor must reluctantly rain on you and your cities.

Therefore, despite your Emperor's never-ending love for you, there really are limits. So reluctantly and unhappily his Imperial Troopers are about to destroy your homes and farms, in order to preserve you from the even more awful doom into which your leaders would plunge you.

You have twenty minutes to get out.

And remember,

YOUR EMPEROR LOVES YOU!

"Run! Run away!" Bill ran toward the house, screaming. "Get out of here!"

Eunice had already read a leaflet, grabbed up a few mementos, and was hurrying out to warn Bill. Together they ran to the road and joined the growing crowd.

Back up the road, out of the valley, they ran. "Run away! Run away!"

They reached Melissa Nafka's house. "Run away!" She was inside, and she hadn't seen the leaflets, but she heard the yelling. Bill saw her flame-colored hair at an upstairs window; it vanished again almost immediately, and moments later the entire woman burst out the front door.

Bill paused in his running to take in the spectacle. Her body fulfilled every promise the house dress had made; that he could see in the seconds before she got her robe wrapped up tightly, covering the leather straps and patent leather hip boots that were all she wore. Behind her came three men, one too old to go into the army, the other two just too young, perhaps a father and his two almost-grown sons, all of them pulling up their pants and swinging shirts gingerly over the welts on their backs.

Bill sighed. Yet another lost glorious opportunity. Perhaps he could return after the Imperial warships had finished obliterating the small community, return and find this woman of his dreams. But for the moment, he had more pressing business.

"Let's get the bowb out of here!"

## CHAPTER 22

BILL COULD STILL HEAR THE BOMBS EXploding when he saw the old stone barn. It had been hit early on, so he figured that maybe it might be safe, if just for a little while. It didn't look like it was really worth bombing twice. He sprinted across the fields to its dilapidated shelter.

Surprisingly, the door was locked. It was so unlikely that Bill tried it again, then rammed it with his shoulder. Neither the lock nor the door was opening and his shoulder hurt.

There was no other choice. Bill, after intense thought, solved the problem. He went around the corner and into the barn through the huge hole in the wall.

In fact, most of the building was gone.

Some of the roof had held together enough to collapse into a kind of lean-to in the far corner, where there were still more or less intact walls, but the only wall that looked whole was the one with the door. Except for the corner where part of it had fallen, the roof was entirely missing. Whatever had been inside, Bill judged from the smell and texture, had either been blown to smith-ereens or made a hasty departure. If anything was still alive in here, it was in that corner lean-to. And it was probably scared and dangerous.

That was the only shelter available.

And Bill wanted it.

It is said that most animals are only truly dangerous when they are cornered, or protecting their young. In an absolute sense, this is largely true. In a relative sense, however, very few animals can be considered dangerous at all under any circumstances if they stand between an irritated Imperial Trooper and his improving his chance of survival. And Bill was decidedly irritated by now.

One of the first bombs had hit Melissa Nafka's house. She probably wouldn't be coming back at all. One of the first cars through the crowd had picked her up, so Bill couldn't follow her in the mass escape.

He had seen where another bomb had hit the local liquor store. Now there was *really* no reason for Bill to stick around.

On the up side, the precision attack had been a first-rate operation. There had been only a few casualties (one of them the older man who had run out of the Nafka place, who tripped on his pants and sprained his knee) while the entire area was rendered incapable of sup-porting human life. Bill had to admire a job well done.

But he would rather admire it in retrospect, and in order to do that he needed some cover.

He strode across the courtyard that had once been a barn, and pounded on what had once been a roof while shouting loudly to announce his presence.

Nothing came out.

That was a good sign.

Unless whatever was inside was too scared to come out.

Bill braced himself for whatever might be waiting and stepped inside the chunk of fallen roof.

It was dark under there, but not so dark that he

couldn't see the many pairs of eyes reflecting the dim light that came in from the sides. They were all together in the darkest corner, and there were enough of them that, whatever they were, they would give Bill more than a little trouble if they decided to attack. He edged away from the opening, to give the glowing eyes a clear shot at the exit, and to give his own eyes a chance to get used to the dark.

The eyes in the corner shifted around; staying as far from him as possible.

Then he heard the sound. It was almost like human whispering; Bill could nearly make out words in it, things that might have been "uniform" and "hiding" and "quiet."

And at last Bill adapted to the dark, before he needed to attack or to defend himself. He could see what faced him.

"Hi, guys," he said.

"Who are you?" one of the men asked.

"Bill." He stepped forward and put out his hand.

"Who are you working for?"

"Eunice Augeas." Bill's hand started to droop.

"Is Eunice on the draft board?"

Before Bill could answer—which was just as well, since he had no idea what they were talking about—another voice said, "No. At least, she didn't used to be."

"I don't think there's a draft board any more," Bill said. "Maybe there's some draft kindling. The whole valley's been blown up pretty good. But what are you talking about?"

"Don't you read the papers?" the first man asked.

Bill considered this, then shook his head. "No."

"Did you hear about the coup?"

"Yup. Actually, I'm on the run from the junta."

"That's okay. So are they. I guess you didn't hear about the other coup?"

Bill blinked. "The other coup?"

"Yeah," said another voice from the back of the barn. "Two guys named Sam and Sid, a couple of days ago. They rescued President Grotsky, rallied the crowds, got the army on their side, and took back control of the government. Heck of a speech they made, standing on that tank."

Bill blinked again. It was the only possible response.

"Anyway, once Grotsky got back in, he announced that the worsening situation gave him no choice—he had to declare martial law. And suspend the constitution. But at least democracy has been restored."

"That's nice," Bill managed to say. "But what about Sam and Sid? What happened to them?"

"Oh, they got shunted off into some dead-end jobs with the Alcoholic Beverage Control Board. Some gratitude, huh?"

"Gee," was all Bill could think of to say. He sat down with a thud among the men in the lean-to.

"So, Bill, what are you doing here? Are you hiding from the draft, too?"

Bill grunted a monosyllabic answer and squinted up at the sky. "Maybe. But I guess you could say I'm more concerned with the rain."

"Rain? It isn't raining."

"Well, things are falling out of the sky, and I'd rather they didn't fall on me."

Now, suddenly, the men gathered around Bill and shook his hand and gripped his shoulder and made other gestures of manly camaraderie. "You're one of us, then, aren't you?"

Bill had been in other situations, once or twice, where a lot of other men were touching him and asking if he was one of them, usually in bars, and the men were usually wrong, but he didn't want to jump to any incorrect conclusions here, since he didn't really feel like having to fight off unwanted advances or leave this ramshackle shelter. So he asked, "One of what?"

"Why, draft dodgers, of course!"

Bill was pretty sure that someone—Betty, for a likely candidate—would have mentioned it before now if there had been conscription in Eyerack. "Is that something new?"

"It's another of President Grotsky's reforms," the apparent leader of the group explained. "Since democracy has been saved, it's important that we all participate fully in our basic freedoms, so everyone between eighteen and thirty-five is being rounded up and trained in unquestioning obedience. It's the only way to preserve our liberties."

"Sure," Bill agreed. "It makes perfect sense."

"And although we support our leaders in every way, we have certain subtle philosophical differences with them on the matter of our being blown into very large numbers of very small pieces."

"I can understand that completely."

Now everyone was able to relax, knowing that no one there would turn them in to the authorities, and that the authorities could not possibly come to get them through the intense bombardment that was turning the surrounding fields of corn and strawberries and kohlrabi into undifferentiated brown muck.

The relatively steady, and relatively distant, thunder of high explosives was oddly reassuring, and they let it become background music to their idle conversation.

Then a man appeared in the entry to the lean-to. Lit only from behind, he seemed hugs. Even Bill found himself intimidated into silence by this apparition.

"Hello!" the stranger said.

After a pause, waiting for someone else to speak, Bill asked, "How did you get here through the bombing?"

"Professional courtesy."

Bill leaped to his feet and ran, bowling the stranger over and making for the ruined walls.

He got only as far as the middle of the barn before the circle of armed men blocked his way. They raised their blasters and clicked off the safeties.

Bill stopped.

The draft dodgers, who had followed him, also stopped, although not before knocking Bill into the mud and manure.

The stranger picked himself up and brushed off the worst of the filth. He pulled a small plastic card out of his shirt pocket and read: "Greetings!" The dodgers moaned. "Your democratically elected president, and loyal elements of the general staff, welcome you to the great adventure of freedom and democracy. In order to preserve human liberties to the fullest, you are hereby inducted into the armed forces of the planet of Eyerack." He put the card away. "Any questions?"

From the back of the crowd, someone put up a hand. One of the guards shot a neat hole through it.

"Bandage that wound. Any other questions?"

There weren't any.

Basic training at Camp Hynline was practically a vacation for Bill. Even though this time it was in an underground shopping mall turned into a boot camp, he'd been through it all before, as a trainee and as an instructor. He could do it in his sleep.

In fact, he did do most of it in his sleep. The officers were especially impressed with his ability to march and follow orders without ever waking up. It was clear he knew what he was doing.

The senior staff met on the matter, and decided that here was a man whose talents, and also whose fangs, should not be wasted. He should be promoted forthwith.

Bill became a sergeant in the Eyerackian army.

He was all in favor of the change. Non-coms in every military force are mostly involved in supervisory activity, which is always preferable to active activity. No one does less work than non-coms, except officers. They also have access to the NCO club; Eyerack was so primitive in its military culture that they served real beer at the NCO club, instead of the recycled near beer at a real Trooper dive. So Bill, true to his optimistic spirit, was inclined to Consider this a good development.

But something did bother him. Perhaps it was a twinge of conscience, or genuine moral curiosity, or a side effect of last night's haggis.

But Bill wondered, was it a conflict of interest to be a member of two opposing armies? Did he owe more loyalty to the Eyerackian army because he had a higher rank here than he did in the Troopers? Or did he owe more to the Troopers because he had sometimes held higher ranks there? Or did he owe more to the Eyerackian because he was already seventeen months overdrawn on his advance pay?

The haggis passed at last, leaving Bill with an unresolved question. He was fully prepared to leave it unresolved, and even to forget it entirely, except as a reminder never to eat haggis again. But fate, as it does so often in an episodic novel, intervened.

Since there was virtually no sign of human life remaining on the surface of the planet, Stormy Wormy Weissearse decided that it was time for a daring and spectacular ground assault.

President Grotsky ordered a total mobilization to stop the enemy advance. Every experienced soldier in the Eyerackian forces must contribute.

The commander of Camp Hynline knew talent when he saw it. Within an hour of the order, Bill had his own squad and was on his way to the front.

## CHAPTER 23

BEING SENT TO THE FRONT HAD THE MOST amazing effect on Bill's morale. Normally the very thought of such a thing would have hurtled him instantly into a deep depression. Now, however, it provided him with the solution to the moral dilemma he had not had time to expunge from his consciousness. Now he knew that it didn't matter which army he was in. They *all* wanted him dead.

He and his squad of raw, untrained, resentful, unedified and undersexed conscripts were passed from officer to officer, working their way down from colonel to lieutenant as surely as they passed from rear echelon to the lines of combat.

At last they reported to Brevet Second Lieutenant Haroun al-Rosenblatt. It was all Hill could do to keep from introducing himself as Brevet Lance Corporal Bill. Except that he was a full sergeant in this army, and they would probably frown on his holding a position in the other army. At the very least, they would stop his pay and put a black mark on his record and shoot him. He really wanted to have a clean record in one army, at least. As well as staying alive.

In civilian life—that is, until mid-afternoon last Tuesday—Rosenblatt had been an artist. He painted flowers mostly, and specialized in murals for large country houses. It was obvious that with this background that when he got called up he was immediately made an officer and assigned to combat intelligence. Bill's squad was assigned to Rosenblatt to replace a squad that the lieutenant had lost the day before. Really lost—he had misplaced them somewhere near the Imperial lines when he stopped to admire a particularly elegant and now-rare example of yarrow, and although he waited for them, they never showed up again.

"Well, Sergeant . . . ?" Rosenblatt frowned and muttered to himself.

"Bill," Bill prompted.

"Oh, yes, it's here in your orders, isn't it? Sergeant Bill. No matter. I'm not going to learn any of your names. You'll all leave me, just like the others . . ." He moaned unhappily and flicked a tear from his eyelash.

"No, sir!" Bill snapped most militarily. "We'll stay with you through thick and thin! We're all loyal soldiers of the—" Not Emperor; that was the other army. What was it here? Oh, yes. "—Republic." He kicked his charges into a chorus of agreement.

"No, no," the officer whined. "None of the soldiers they send me stay for long. They get captured, or they run away, or they get killed, but none of them ever come back from patrol. I don't even deserve to be in the army . . ."

"None of us do, sir," Bill reassured him. "But that is the way of the world. So here we all are, and we have to work together, don't we?" He put an arm around Rosenblatt's shaking shoulders. "Of course we'll come back. We're highly trained professional soldiers; these boys have even been through over a week of boot camp. We'll get out there and bring back all the intelligence you need." He kicked out at the squad, but they had shown their eagerness to learn by moving out of range. Bill had to resort to language an officer was sure to understand. "Trust me," he implied.

Lieutenant Rosenblatt hesitantly wiped another tear from the corner of one eye. "Well, all right . . . If you say so . . ." He looked over his troops. "I must say, you're a fine-looking bunch of lads. Well, let's get going . . ."

Bill put one hand on his commander's chest, nearly covering it completely. "Why don't you tell us what the mission is?" he suggested firmly.

"Oh. I guess that's a good idea We're supposed to go out there . . ." He waved vaguely toward the enemy lines. ". . . and find out what's going on, and where the enemy is, and all . . ."

"May I make a suggestion, sir?"

"Oh? I guess so . . ."

"You're much too valuable to risk on a routine reconnaissance. I've had much more experience with this sort of thing. I think you should stay here and plan our strategy, and we'll just wander out and have a look around. And be back with the information in no time. That way you can have plenty of time to think about our next orders. Okay?"

"Well, I not sure that's that's a good idea . . ."

"Sir. You can follow us with your field glasses." Bill fixed Rosenblatt with a baleful glare. "Trust me." He bared his fangs.

A desultory artillery barrage from both sides had given no-man's land a familiar agricultural texture. So far that had been the biggest problem they'd faced; the men in Bill's squad kept tripping over stones and clods. Though they were starting to look like well-grimed veterans they still hadn't seen any action.

Though normally armed conflict was something better avoided, Bill had worked up a dubious plan that sort of depended on their seeing some action. For this reason he had tried getting closer to the Imperial lines, and in one impetuous moment had even waved at some of the troopers, but no one shot at him. Or waved back. He couldn't risk shooting at them; they might take it seriously and really try to kill him. Instead of simply firing their weapons to show their officers they were still awake. But maybe he could get something going if he called in the Eyerackian artillery.

"Lieutenant," he whispered into the wrist radio Rosenblatt had given him.

There was no response.

"Lieutenant Rosenblatt," he whispered a little louder. Nothing.

He tried again, in a normal speaking voice.

Still nothing.

"Yo! Bowb-head!" he screamed. Way off in the distance, he could see the lieutenant jump. "Sir?" Bill whispered.

"Yes, Sergeant? Did you want me, or anything . . . ?"

"We've gotten about as close to the enemy lines as we can right now, but there's something I'd like to get a better look at. I might be able to identify the units we're facing if I could get in closer."

"Well, I don't know what I can do to help . . ."

"I need artillery cover, sir."

"Artillery cover, Sergeant? I don't know about that . . ."

Step by step, Bill explained to the lieutenant how to call in an artillery strike. He took a careful reading of his own position, and told Rosenblatt, "Make sure they aim at these exact coordinates. If they aim exactly there, we'll be safe."

Sure enough, in a few minutes shells were landing all around them, everywhere but on the spot where Bill told his squad to stay put.

Bill started to edge forward through the tumult, keeping one eye on the incoming artillery and one on the enemy lines. Very quickly, this became too much for anyone who wasn't wall-eyed, so he just watched the shells.

As soon as he saw one that looked like it was going to land just in front of him, he started running forward as hard as he could. He dove forward at the last instant, and the shock wave carried him up and into the Imperial trenches, where he landed in the arms of several very surprised troopers.

"Hi, guys," he said. "I'm home."

Nobody knew quite what to make of the strange soldier who had appeared in the very front lines. He was wearing Eyerackian insignia, which would make him a prisoner of war, or maybe a defector. But he was also wearing what looked like an Imperial Trooper uniform, which would make him a deserter. But the uniform was clearly a fake, being much too sturdy and well-tailored, which made him a spy. To be safe, they clapped him in irons and sent him to the rear. He smiled all the way.

Bill tried to explain, really he did. He told them, "I'm a prisoner. A P.O.W." And they would say, "Of course you are, we just captured you," and he would claim that they hadn't captured him, he had come voluntarily, and they would say that didn't matter, and he would say he was a prisoner, and the whole round would start all over again.

What was important to Bill, of course, was that he was getting farther and farther away from the fighting, and, perhaps even more important, closer and closer to his foot locker.

That had been, in the final analysis, the final element that made up his mind. He had been wearing the Swiss Army Foot for a long time now without a break, and there were no replacements on Eyerack. If he was ever going to get a change of foot, he would somehow have to get back to Camp Buboe. And the first step in that was to get back into the Troopers.

Besides, if he was going to have to go into combat, he'd rather cut down on the chances of being accidentally shot by his own side, and the chances of that looked pretty good in the Eyerackian forces.

So Bill struggled happily in his chains, creating more and more of an administrative problem, until each officer in turn bucked him up the chain of command, and further toward the rear.

Of course, each officer also insisted that more chains be added, so he couldn't be accused of not doing anything about the situation. By the time he was taken out of the colonel's office, the MPs were wheeling him on a hand truck.

At last, utterly immobilized, invisible except for part of his face, rolling along on a machinery dolly, but still smiling like a head case, Bill was wheeled into the Presence.

"Hi, sir! I'm home!"

General Weissearse turned slowly and peered at the mass of chromed steel before him.

"By the Lord above, I know that voice!"

The general tried to push aside some of the coils of chain to see Bill's face more clearly, but there were too many.

"Remove this man's chains at once!"

Adjutants, aides, guards, and everyone else in the room jumped to execute the general's order. A fist fight broke out just on Bill's left, as two officers and a non-com vied to unshackle Bill's leg. The non-com decked the captain with one punch, but collapsed when the lieutenant caught her in the solar plexus with a kick. Most of the action was more of the wrestling variety, however, and Bill got thrown around quite a bit in the process.

One by one, the chains were unlocked and lifted away, gradually revealing God's own tail gunner. At least, Bill hoped he would be recognized as God's own tail gunner by God's own general.

He was not disappointed.

"*You!*" General Weissearse said.

Bill spread his arms wide. "I have returned!"

"Put that man in chains!" the general ordered.

Putting the chains back on was even more difficult than getting them off; Bill wasn't nearly so cooperative this time. But the results were about the same. Bill was soon completely wrapped in chains again.

"What have you got to say for yourself?"

"Mmrrgm ffmrff hmmff. Mm nrrrnf ffrrm mrrffm. Mrggnff!"

"What language is this man speaking? Get a transla-tor!" the general ordered.

Almost everyone in the room below the rank of full colonel stampeded for the door, each one claiming to know what language it was and someone who could translate.

The non-com who'd been knocked down earlier, and was just now getting up, probably couldn't have made it to the door in competitive time in any case, but she did have an alternate suggestion. "He's got a mouth full of steel. Take off the chain around his head."

General Weissearse shouted, "Halt!" The stampede stopped. "Why don't we just remove the chain from his head?"

"Terrific idea, General," said a colonel.

"Great idea, sir," said a major.

"Brilliant thinking, General," said a captain.

"You leave me in utter awe, sir," said a lieutenant.

"*My* bowing idea," muttered a sergeant.

"Sergeant, remove the chain!" General Weissearse proclaimed.

She did it smartly, twirling the end of the chain off with a flip that snapped it neatly against the back of Bill's skull.

"Now, Bill, what have you got to say for yourself?"

Bill swayed slightly, and tried to pick out which of the generals he was seeing was the real one. Weissearse always looked a little like hallucination, so it wasn't an easy choice, but they were all standing pretty close together, so it wasn't an important choice either.

"Brevet Lance Corporal Bill, reporting for duty, *sir*!" Bill tried to salute, but he could only rattle his chains slightly. He was already immovably at attention.

"Hah! That's what you say! But tell us, Deserter Bill, *Traitor* Bill, why are you wearing Eyerackian Army insignia on your uniform? And where's your real uniform? This is an obvious forgery."

"It looks just the same," Bill protested.

"It's an obvious case of *lèse-officier*. This uniform is made out of real cloth, not recycled paper."

"I couldn't help it," Bill whimpered. "They took it away from me in the hospital."

"Aha! Accepting aid and comfort from the enemy, too! On top of desertion." The general wheeled and pointed to three of the officers in the room. "You, you, and you. What do you say?"

The three officers looked at each other in abject terror, praying that one of the others would speak first. Finally one of them decided that a wrong answer was less dangerous than no answer.

"Splunge!" he said.

"Splunge?" spluttered the general. "What kind of a verdict is that? I want guilty or not guilty!"

"Guilty!"

"Guilty!"

"Guilty!"

"Oh, yes sir, really guilty."

"Very guilty."

"Extremely guilty!"

"Enough!" General Weissearse turned back to Bill. "Well, Bill, you've been given a fair trial and found guilty of desertion and a bunch of other things we'll fill in later when we do the paperwork. Do you have anything to say for yourself?"

Bill didn't have to think about this one. "I'm too young to die!" he groaned.

"Son," the general said paternally, putting one hand gently on Bill's head (he couldn't find a shoulder under all the chains), "that isn't one of the choices.

"May the Lord bless you, my boy. Okay, soldiers, take him out and shoot him."

The MPs started to wrestle Bill back onto the dolly.

A thin gray man in a gray trench coat appeared, possibly out of a cabinet, because Bill hadn't seen him before and only saw him now because he was too trussed up to struggle, and whispered a few words in the general's ear. The general actually seemed to listen to him. They whispered back and forth for a couple of minutes.

Bill had time to watch all this, because the MPs were having a lot of trouble balancing him on the dolly; he kept falling off, and only the thick layer of chains kept him from a serious injury, which he would have appreciated a lot more if he weren't about to die. But at last they got him propped up and started to wheel him out.

"Wait!" intoned the general. "Bill, would you like a chance to redeem yourself?"

The assembled headquarters staff gasped in astonishment.

"Sure," Bill said. "Do I get to stay alive?"

"No."

"Do I get to stay alive a little longer?"

"Yes."

It was another easy choice. "What do I have to do?"

# CHAPTER 24

WHILE WAITING FOR THE FINAL COUNT-down, Bill ran over his equipment list one more time.

Suicide pill—check.

Teeny-tiny little radio transmitter disguised as a cock-roach—check.

Yup, he had it all.

Now all he had to do was wait.

He didn't exactly know what he was waiting for. He'd never traveled by onager before. It was something very old-fashioned, which probably meant that it was usually reserved for the nobility, but so far it didn't feel all that comfortable.

The MPs had removed the chains, which was more comfortable than wearing them, and which certainly made a secret suicide mission a lot easier to accomplish. But the MPs were still standing there, on the platform above him, with their blasters aimed right at some of his favorite body parts.

Riding the onager, whatever it was, seemed to involve waiting in a big bowl. He was lying in the bowl now.

It also seemed to involve some risk; he was wearing a backpack that was some kind of automatic device. The man in the gray trench coat had told him that Bill didn't have to know how to work it, at any rate.

So Bill just lay there and waited until an officer stuck his head up over the edge of the big bowl and said, "Ready to go?"

"Ready for final countdown, sir!"

"Countdown? Oh, all right. Five four three two one, go!" He pulled his head back and signaled to someone below. Bill heard an axe cut through something, and then he was airborne.

Aside from the surprise of it, being flung from a catapult was interesting, even pleasant. There was nothing between Bill and the pure experience of flight, no vehicle, not even a protective outfit like the commando suits. It was just Bill and the air, as he sped up over the battlefield among the surviving birds.

And then, after a little while of soaring up, he reached the top of his arc and started to go down.

For future reference, Bill noted that flapping his arms like a bird's wings was of no use whatsoever. Nor was praying. He already knew that whimpering did no good.

He began to wonder if the device in the backpack was a bomb or something. It seemed like a lot of trouble to go to, just to make him dead. Maybe it was a now experimental method of execution, as though the military needed one.

He had been instructed to curl up into a ball once he started descending, and he actually remembered to do it once he'd exhausted his other options. It was something about reducing his radar profile, so he'd look like just another artillery shell. Bill didn't think it would do much for his chances for survival, but they were so close to nil that it didn't make any difference. While he was curled into the fetal position anyway, he stuck his thumb in his mouth too, for old times' sake. It had been reassuring once.

This time it nearly cost him his front teeth.

A few feet from the ground (as far as he could tell with his eyes squeezed shut), there was a singularly unpleasant crunching-wrenching sensation in his back. He came to a sudden stop.

In a few tiny fractions of a second, the antigravity generator in the pack stopped Bill in mid-plummet; fireworks blew out the back of the pack, simulating the landing of a shell in a small fireworks depot. At the same time the straps of the pack retracted, dropping Bill the last ten feet to the ground. Its mission accomplished, the pack gently lowered itself to the field, where tiny automatic shovels popped out and quickly buried it.

Bill pulled himself up, brushed off the worst of the mud, and looked around. It seemed that no one had noticed his arrival. He threw out the suicide pill and checked the bug. It still looked like a cockroach; its little legs and antennae worked away inside its glass tube.

Now he had to figure out where he was. The little gray man had assured Bill that he would land somewhere near the Eyerackian headquarters, where he was supposed to plant the tiny robot transmitter.

He looked carefully around. There was an opening in the ground, not far away, that reminded Bill of the entrance to the neutron mine. It was about the same size, but it was much busier. There were staff hovercars and trucks and people going in and out pretty steadily. The big doors hardly got a chance to close. Since this was the only structure in sight, aside from a few trenches and a couple of outhouses, Bill decided it was the best candidate for enemy headquarters. And if he got in there it would surely provide some shelter if the Troopers decided to start serious shelling to disguise his arrival.

Bill attached himself to the end of a column of marching soldiers that was headed inside. The officer at the head of the line was questioned, but the rest of them were waved right in, right past the sign at the entrance: TRULY DEMOCRATIC AND FREE ARMY OF

THE GENUINELY DEMOCRATIC AND REPUB-
LICAN PLANET OF EYERACK—Secret Military
Headquarters. This was it, all right!

The column halted in a big room, and the officer gave
the command to count off. Bill had to do some quick
thinking. The officer must have had a record of how
many soldiers had come in with him. That number
would have to match the last number that was counted
off. So in order to make the count come out right, Bill
would either have to not give a number at all—but the
person in front of him in the formation would notice
that—or give the same number as the person before him,
which he figured was much less likely to be noticed.

Bill was being a model soldier, eyes riveted in front,
so he couldn't see much of what was going on. He
noticed that the soldier in front of him needed a haircut;
the Eyerackian army must be pretty disorganized, he
thought, if they couldn't even shave every conscript's
head. He also noticed that a lot of the voices in the room
were kind of high-pitched; it was a shame that they had
had to start drafting young boys, he thought.

Then it was almost his turn. The soldier in front of
him piped, "Forty-five!"

In his best military style, Bill boomed out, "Forty-
five!" That should fool them.

There was complete silence for a moment. Then Bill
could hear the officer's boots walking slowly the length
of the room, coming down to the end of the line, to
Bill. He kept his eyes locked straight out.

"Right, *face!*" The order came from very near by.

Bill executed a perfect turn, moving only his feet. His
view now included the top of an officerial hat.

"What are *you* doing here?" the officer demanded.

"Sergeant Bill, reporting for duty, *sir!*"

"I know who you are, you silly sausage. What made
you think you could pose as one of my soldiers? Did
you do this just to find me? How sweet!"

This didn't sound like any officer Bill had ever met

before. He allowed himself to look down. "Calyfigia!"

She pointed to her collar. "Major Calyfigia, to you, buster. At least while we're on duty."

Bill looked around. Not only was he the tallest soldier in the room by at least half a foot, he was the only man.

"What kind of unit is this?" Bill asked.

"The Third Volunteer Housewife Commandos," Major Calyfigia said proudly. "Ready to defend hearth and home by assassinating the enemy. We infiltrate, posing as cleaning ladies, then plant bear-traps and bombs. But here I am chattering away, when I know President Grotsky must be dying to see you."

All the way down through the warren of the headquarters, Calyfigia told him at exhausting length how the invasion had changed her whole outlook on the war. Basically, she had become a bloodthirsty, gung-ho warrior, out for vengeance. In husky tones she confided how Bill was now one of her heroes. "If you're free later, I'd like to discuss various forms of hand-to-hand combat with you," she said with a sultry wink when she left him at the door to the war room.

Fortunately, Bill was used to being confused. He didn't bother telling Calyfigia that he was scheduled to be dead later. Nothing else ever happened on schedule, so maybe they might get together.

Noise came pouring out of the war room when Bill opened the door. People were shouting updated information, calling for files, discussing foreplay, screaming orders over the phones, and arguing over strategy, while a small swing band was playing in one corner. Bill stepped into the room, and it suddenly fell silent. Even the band broke off in the middle of "Boogie Woogie Synthesizer Boy." Everyone was staring at Bill.

"Hi, guys," he said. "I'm home!"

Millard Grotsky, wearing a field marshal's uniform, slowly rose from his desk and stared at Bill. "We were told you were dead."

"Nope," Bill said with a smile. "Almost, but not quite."

"Good," Grotsky said. "Very good. That means we can put you on trial for desertion!"

Bill didn't have any ready answers for that one, since by a strictly technical interpretation, what he had done—running away from this side during combat to join the other side—could be seen as desertion.

"I need three volunteers!" Grotsky declared. Nobody moved. "To be judges, that's all." A forest of hands went up.

Within minutes a space had been cleared in the middle of the war room, with the president's desk at one end and a folding chair for Bill at the other. The three judges sat on one side.

President Grotsky stood up. "Officers of the court, ladies and gentlemen. I'd like to welcome you all to our very first court-martial here in the freedom-loving, democratic, and law-abiding Republic of Eyerack. If I may, I'd like to open the proceedings with a short statement."

He pointed a finger at Bill. "That man deserted from the army. He ought to be shot. Thank you. What is your verdict?"

The judges looked at each other. The one in the middle said, "Sounds good to me," and shrugged.

"Okay."

"Yeah."

"Can we go back to work now?" the first one asked.

"I object!" Bill objected.

"Why should you object if we go back to work?" the second judge asked.

"No, I object to the trial."

The third judge said, "We had a trial. What more do you want?"

"Don't I get a chance to defend myself?"

The judges looked at President Grotsky for guidance.

"Gee, Bill, we've never had a court-martial before.

Are you supposed to get a lawyer or something?"

"Of course. When I had my court-martial in the Troopers, even they let me get a lawyer and defend myself."

"Hmm." Grotsky conferred with a couple of his aides. "No, we haven't got any lawyers handy. Sent them all up with the combat units since everyone agreed that they would never be missed. But I guess we can let you speak for yourself. Speak." He leaned back to listen.

"Not guilty, I am sure." Bill needed to think fast and that had never been his strong point. This, being a case of life or death, however really started his braincells ticking over. "First off I'm not a citizen of Eyerack. I'm actually a citizen of the Empire, so in order to be free to join your army, I had to go back to the Empire and renounce my citizenship. Then I came back right away. How's that?"

"Not bad for a quick improvisation," Grotsky said. "Judges?"

One of the judges worked at a computer. The computer buzzed loudly. "I'm sorry. You have to be a citizen to be drafted, but according to our records you volunteered. See?" He swiveled the screen around so Bill and the others could see the copy of Bill's file, where "drafted" had been neatly crossed out and changed to "volunteered."

"I better try again." Bill racked his brain until he remembered something from his first trial. "You declared martial law, right?" President Grotsky conceded that. "So the whole planet is like a military base, and I never left the planet, so I couldn't have deserted. Right?"

The third judge raised his hand. "Can I have this one?" The president nodded his assent. "When you were last seen by Lieutenant Rosenblatt you were airborne after an explosion. As far as we can tell, you dropped out of the sky near these headquarters some time later. You were definitely off the surface of the planet for some part of that time. Still guilty."

"It's a frameup," Bill whined. "I can't be a deserter because I'm actually a member of the Imperial Troopers, so I was actually reporting to my unit for duty." He looked around cautiously. When there was no immediate response he started to smile a smirky smile.

"I like it," pronounced the president. "I like it a lot."

"By George, I think he's got it," said the first judge after they had had a chance to discuss it.

"He has indeed. He's done it," said the second.

"Absolutely," said the third. "He is not guilty of desertion." There was a smattering of applause. "He is not a deserter. He's a spy. *Guilty!*"

"Excellent," enthused Grotsky. "Take him out and shoot him!"

A pair of MPs grabbed Bill and started moving him toward the door. They got him about halfway there before the president called out, "Stop!"

Grotsky was talking with a gray figure who had appeared on a holoscreen behind him.

"Snorri!" Bill shouted. "Snorri! Save me!"

"Too late, Bill," Grotsky intoned. "Snorri Yakamoto turned out to be a cleverly disguised Chinger spy. He disappeared before we could shoot him. This is Bodger Portcullis, my new covert operations adviser. Say hello, Bodger."

"Gee, Bill," Bodger said, "it looks like you're in a real pickle, huh?"

Bill was struck speechless by an MP's hand over his mouth.

"Suppose we let you go on a suicide mission instead of shooting you? Would you like that?"

Grotsky nodded, as though encouraging Bill to agree. Since Bill had been on suicide missions before—and was on one now, in fact—he figured he might as well go along. He nodded too.

# CHAPTER 25

BODGER MAY HAVE BEEN A NEW ADDITION to Grotsky's intelligence staff (Bill heard one of the other spies complain, "We don't need no stinkin' Bodger"), but his idea was pretty familiar.

Bill had spent the last few minutes being lashed to a ballista. Unlike the onager, which was a giant catapult, the ballista was a fairly high-tech piece of machinery. It was a giant crossbow, and what Bill was actually going to be riding was the javelin it would launch. The idea was that this would make him look just like an artillery shell to the radar. He would land near Trooper head-quarters and plant a small transmitter, cleverly disguised as an empty toilet paper roll, which would send a hom-ing signal for an Eyerackian missile.

"How's the countdown going?" Bill asked the tech-nician in charge of the ballista, not really liking any of this.

"What countdown?" The technician pulled a lever.

*Whoosh!*

Bill had never really considered projectiles in much

detail. Most of the weapons he used were either energy weapons, like blasters, or guided missiles, like the TAIL GUNNER! smart missiles. He had never thought about the problems of hitting a target with something that just lobbed out and flew through the air. He might never have come up with the principle of gyroscopic stabilization on his own, had he not been experiencing it.

Gyroscopic stabilization means that if something is spinning around its long axis, it will keep going straight. The faster it spins, the more accurate its flight will be.

The javelin felt as though it was going to be very accurate.

Bill couldn't really tell, though, because when it hit, releasing the straps that held him fast, it was all he could do to throw himself to the ground. And he almost missed.

The sky was spinning around him, so he rolled over. Then the ground was spinning, so he closed his eyes. They were spinning too, but he couldn't stand the thought of opening them again.

But eventually the universe and Bill came to rest with respect to each other, and he could try to figure out where he was. Which was just behind the Imperial lines, not very far from the headquarters.

Bill knew what he had to do.

He checked through a few foxholes for the rawest recruits he could find. There! Those would do—Fall young, all buck privates, all scared to death. All bright green with fear.

Bill jumped into the middle of the group, grabbed a blaster rifle, and said in his best drillfield voice, "Don't tell me that you bowb-heads are scared? Come on—there's a war going on here that sure needs fighting!"

He leaped out and started charging across the trenches toward the Eyerackian lines. As he crossed each trench, he shouted more encouragement. "Don't be cowards! Attack! Attack! Do this for your Emperor—and your mothers too!"

He stood on top of the last trench, struck a heroic pose, waved his rifle over his head, and called, "DEATH OR GLORY!" And he charged out alone into the battlefield.

When he estimated he was about halfway across he started looking carefully around him. Little puffs of vaporized dirt were starting to be blasted into the air. If he angled just a little to the left, about fifty feet ahead—

Arrgh! Bill fell headfirst down into a deep shell hole. He couldn't be seen from either side as long as he stayed in here and kept his head down. Which was easy enough to do since he was jammed in. It was what Bill always dreamed of—safe. Now he could have some nice quiet time to think about what to do next.

Whatever he thought he would do next, he was wrong. A peculiar noise was building behind him. It sounded almost like . . . No, that couldn't be. But it did sound very much like thousands of troopers charging across a field.

And that's exactly what it turned out to be. A wave of them, stampeding toward the enemy lines, trampling everything in their path into the mud.

When Bill awoke in the hospital he was as thoroughly encased in bandages as he had once been in chains. He wasn't sure which one was better. In either case, he couldn't move and he could barely talk. He could still feel bootprints on some of his more personal body parts as well as the soles of his feet. Had the whole army stepped on him? He couldn't remember anything after the assault wave reached his shell hole. He wasn't even certain whose hospital he was in. And asking someone could be awkward, when each side had sentenced him to death for deserting to the other.

He lay there for a while, staring at the ceiling. If he'd been able to move, he might have turned on the holovision, but he couldn't even turn his head to find out if there was one there. All in all, it was only a very little bit better than being dead.

Eventually a nurse came to change his catheter. This was extremely painful, and cheered Bill up considerably. In a matter like this, Bill was of the belief that pain, which would eventually go away, was much better than numbness, which might not.

He also got a glimpse of the nurse. She looked enough like General Weissearse that Bill suspected at first that it was him in drag. But the nurse had more of a mustache than the general, as well as being much more masculine. She also had Imperial Trooper nurses' insignia on her shoulders, with the familiar slogan, "Nurse till it hurts!" So now he knew where he was. Fatigue and blackness overwhelmed him.

The next time he became aware of a nurse, he started moaning, as any good Trooper would, to indicate that he was barely restraining his screams of agony. This impressed the female staff, according to legend, and sometimes led to the administration of massages or psychoactive medication. (Bill had spent a lot of time in hospitals in his military career, and this ploy had never yet worked; such is the hold of myth on the human imagination, however, that he still tried it every time.)

Imagine his surprise when the nurse actually came over! She checked his chart for a part of his body that wasn't too badly injured, then stroked his forehead gently and said, "There, there, now. Is the pain too horrible to bear?" Bill nodded, by way of indicating that he was in too much pain to speak. "Well, we can't have you moaning like that. You're going to get a visitor! Here, just bite down on this."

She slipped something into his mouth and left. Bill examined the something with his teeth and tongue. It wasn't quite the right shape for a pill; one end of it was rounded, but the other end was flat. He tapped it gently with his teeth; it was hard.

A bullet. She'd given him a bullet to bite. And he was

too bandaged up to take it out of his mouth.

But the nurse said something about a visitor, didn't she? That was a little puzzle. Bill didn't know anyone in the entire Imperial armada, unless you counted General Weissearse, and if he knew Bill was here he would just send an execution squad.

It just shows how wrong you can be. Bill recognized the sound of the general's staff toadying down the ward long before the general reached his bed.

"So, here's our hero, eh? You must be in the good graces of the Lord, my son, to have survived that marvelous attack you led. Does anybody here know this man's name? Can't see a blessed thing with all these bandages."

Bill maneuvered the bullet between his teeth, and decided not to identify himself. He moaned a little bit to appear more heroic.

"No matter. You're a tremendous inspiration to us all, my boy. Single-handedly you stimulated our men to think of victory—not death for a change—then led them in an attack against hopeless odds, with no thought to your own safety, a fighting fool who inspired the troops to follow you into the very jaws of death! The fact that most of them were killed in no way detracts from your achievement.

"To honor your courage and leadership, and on behalf of the Emperor, I'd like to present you with—what medals have we got handy?"

An aide came up with a small box, and the general rummaged around for a moment.

"Yes, that's a nice one. I'd like to present you with the Order of the Galactic Jakes. You should know that this also entitles you to one free drink in the officer's club of your choice, if you ever become an officer, which is very unlikely."

The general pinned the medal onto Bill personally; fortunately, Bill had the bullet to bite on as the pin pierced his flesh.

"Now, son, is there anything else we can do for you?"

Bill swallowed the bullet so he could speak clearly. "Yes, sir! I'd like a new foot!" He waggled his right leg in illustration.

"Consider it done!" said Weissearse. "Doctor, see to it that there's a regulation human foot at the end of that leg right away!"

Bill sighed. His dream was about to come true.

Within minutes, orderlies came in to prepare him for surgery and wheel him down to the operating room. In what seemed like no time—probably because he was unconscious most of the time—Bill was back in the ward, back in his bed.

He awoke slowly, relishing the anesthesia, stretching his legs, flexing his feet. That woke him up fully. He flexed his right foot. It felt just like a foot! He curled his right toes. They felt just like toes!

"Nurse! Nurse!"

The nurse came running, with the doctor right behind her. "Is something wrong? Are you in pain?"

"My foot! My foot!" Bill was almost too excited to speak.

"Your foot hurts?" the doctor asked. "That's normal after surgery, but it'll go away."

"No! No!" Bill took a breath and tried to relax. "Let me see my foot!"

"Ah!"

The doctor carefully unwrapped the bandages at the bottom of Bill's right leg. Bill could see a glimpse of pink, human flesh through the gauze. The nurse held his head up so he would watch the complete unveiling.

"*Voilà!*" With a flourish, the doctor twirled the last wrapping off.

Bill was speechless. There, at the end of his right leg, was a foot, a real foot, a human foot—a very familiar foot.

He looked at it more closely. It was a left foot. Well, never mind, at least it was a *foot*.

"What do you think?" the doctor asked.

"It's lovely," Bill said. "At last I have two feet again."

The doctor looked embarrassed. "Not exactly."

Bill's joy started to evaporate. "How not exactly?" he grated.

"Well, the general wanted you to have a foot on the end of your leg there, what we medical men call an *ankle*, but there's a chronic shortage of feet. I guess you know all about that. Anyway, the only place we could find a foot to put on your right leg was, well, your left leg. I'm sure that you will like that foot, for you have had it a long time. That's your own left foot."

Bill's grated out a murderous oath so awful that the doctor's body temperature fell ten degrees and he almost swooned. Then Bill screamed. "What's on my left leg, then?"

"You'll like it, I'm sure that you will. It's a very nice piece of work, if I say so myself," the doctor said as he unwrapped the bandages with numb fingers and chattering teeth. "And quite handy, too, I think you could say."

Bill screamed again, Where his left foot used to be, before it became his right foot, there was a hand. A particularly ugly, hairy hand. It had thick dirty nails and a tattoo across the back, saying DEATH TO ALL CHINGERS.

He formed the hand into a fist and swung it at the doctor and decked him with a neat uppercut. The nurses dragged the doctor away.

"You'll get used to it," the doctor moaned. "It's really quite distinctive." He kept reassuring Bill as they carried him out of the ward.

The foot transplant healed nicely, but it took Bill a while to get used to walking on his new hand. He tried walking on his fingertips, flat or balled into a fist. All of these were most uncomfortable. He was only happy when he could make a fist of his hand-foot and swing at the doctor when he passed. The doctor avoided him so Bill hobbled-walked around the hospital looking for him. Ready to drop on his back and swing a fist whenever he found him.

On one of his expeditions, he paused for a rest in front of the bulletin board. New notices were the only reading material available. And Bill looked them over lethargically.

YOUR EMPEROR LOVES YOU!
*"Yes, I do I really do!"*
What follows is a real live quote from The Emperor.

The Emperor and the General Staff would like to thank all the enlisted men and women of his valiant and glorious armed forces for their generous required voluntary contributions to the Emperor's Birthday Present Fund.

Your participation made it possible to buy, for the Emperor, something he has always wanted: a brain transplant that might raise his IQ above 35. You should be pleased that merely foregoing one week's pay has made so much pleasure possible.

Bill wondered if that was one of the weeks he'd been a prisoner of Eyerack. That made him wonder if he would get his back pay for serving in the Eyerackian army. He guessed not. He probably forfeited all of his back pay when he was sentenced to death. There was another notice.

YOUR EMPEROR LOVES YOU!
"Yes, I do, I really do!"—The Emperor.
The Imperial Household Staff announces with great regret that tragedy has once again struck the beloved Imperial Family.

Due to inherited circulatory troubles it has been

discovered that Grand Admiral Kvetch of the Imperial Navy has been braindead for six years. All of his recent orders are canceled.

The poor man, Bill commiserated. He had served under other officers who were braindead and it never seemed to impede their performance. Or improve it. But of course it was more serious when a relative of the Emperor got it.

There were other Imperial edicts, but Bill was too depressed to read them. He made his way slowly back to his solitary bed, seeing the doctor once on the way and swinging a foot-fist that almost got him. He hit the wall instead and put a hole in it. At times he was beginning to enjoy his third hand, although he really would have preferred a foot if there had been any choice.

He sat on the edge of his bed trimming his toenails with his new hand. Handy. But depressing.

As were the Troopers and the whole war and everything. He would be well soon and out of the hospital and back in the front lines. If he didn't think of something fast.

He couldn't think of something even slow, which was even more depressing. He turned on the holovision and skipped through the channels. All ads. Including one asking for volunteers for the Recruiting Service. A busty blond in a tight uniform was touting for the military.

"We need men with guts. Men who are not afraid to serve their Emperor out there at the ragged ends of the Empire. Men ready to recruit the soldiers needed to fight this war to end all wars.

"This is a specialized occupation that fills a specific need. Combat veterans are asked to apply. Especially wounded ones not fit to fight very much more. Serve your Emperor. This is an equal opportunity job. It doesn't matter if you have tusks and two right arms and three hands. Your Emperor needs you!"

"He certainly does," Bill sighed, shaking hands with himself and bending over so he could twang his tusks with his free hand.

The timeless saga of Bill, the Galactic Hero, was drawing to a reluctant end.

The saga of Bill, the Recruiting Sergeant, was about to begin.

THE END

# ARTHUR C. CLARKE'S VENUS PRIME™

## by Paul Preuss

**VOLUME 6: THE SHINING ONES** 75350-2/$3.95 US/$4.95 CAN
The ever capable Sparta proves the downfall of the mysterious and sinister organization that has been trying to manipulate human history.

**VOLUME 5: THE DIAMOND MOON**
75349-9/$3.95 US/$4.95 CAN
Sparta's mission is to monitor the exploration of Jupiter's moon, Amalthea, by the renowned Professor J.Q.R. Forester.

**VOLUME 4: THE MEDUSA ENCOUNTER**
75348-0/$3.95 US/$4.95 CAN
Sparta's recovery from her last mission is interrupted as she sets out on an interplanetary investigation of her host, the Space Board.

**VOLUME 3: HIDE AND SEEK** 75346-4/$3.95 US/$4.95 CAN

**VOLUME 2: MAELSTROM** 75345-6/$4.50 US/$5.50 CAN

**VOLUME 1: BREAKING STRAIN** 75344-8/$3.95 US/$4.95 CAN

Each volume features a special technical infopak,
including blueprints of the structures of *Venus Prime*